GOLDEN ROSE

and other stories

Ben Starling

EDINGTON
PRESS

Edington Press

Paperback ISBN: 978-0-9565812-8-0
Kindle ISBN: 978-0-9565812-9-7

www.benstarlingauthor.com

For Toby and Lara

ACKNOWLEDGEMENTS

This novella and short stories have benefitted from helpful feedback from a number of kind people including Robin Alcott, Linda Alton, members of the Facebook MR James Appreciation Society, and members of Excalibur Advanced Toastmasters (Public Speaking) Club, London, UK.

I am very grateful to graphic designer Gregg Stockdale for creating the wonderful cover. He can be contacted at: sludgieboy@googlemail.com.

WHAT GOODREADS AND AMAZON READERS ARE SAYING ABOUT BEN'S WRITING

"Reading the author's elegant prose, you can almost taste the saltwater, feel the sand between your toes, hear the birds in the jungle and smell the warm, damp earth. But there is also something strange, otherworldly, about it. The only book that I have read which in places has a similar feel is The Story Teller by the great Mario Vargas Llosa. I cannot think of any higher praise than that." ~ Rassendyl

"The author has created a thought provoking and wonderful adventure that packs a powerful punch. Simple clear truths rise elegantly from this tightly written plot in a world you can almost touch. I like the precise economy of words that creates verdant scenery in a few well-dealt phrases. I enjoy the rhythm, the imagery, the unexpected alliteration. But what I really like best is its rising pace and the tight feeling of imminent potential we find throughout..." ~ BBLM

"Beautifully written, with a musical cadenza that alternates perfectly timed dialogue and exquisitely crafted descriptive passages…I sighed with deep regret as I turned the last page, transfixed by a world I couldn't bear to leave..."
~ Indefinible

"I really can't say enough about how incredible Starling's writing is and how powerful this tale is. This is superb quality from beginning to end; there is no skimping on plot or words within. Absolutely one of the best books I've read!"
~ Jennifer L

"Ben Starling has a true gist to make fiction real in the imagination as well as impart some very important facts and messages" ~ Lindi

"Well written, completely engaging with characters you can reach out and touch (and want to love, like, kick)." ~ Lilyana
"I have to say that I have never cried so long over the last few chapters of a book as I did with this - tears of great sadness and tears of great joy." ~ ML Downs

"Well written, great story, love the important message portrayed through the characters and their journey. Romance, spiritualism, myths. mystery, fantasy, breaking and entering, murder all fitted together with care. wonderful descriptions and diverse characters." ~ Jenni

"I couldn't put it down. I found myself putting off important jobs just to read a few pages more! I laughed and cried at times (such was the depth that I had immersed myself into the story) and not many books do that to me." ~ Soughton

"The writing is excellent and gripping from the outset. The descriptions of locations both onshore and off are very evocative." ~ OutandBack

"Starling knows how to tell a story and doesn't hold back when it comes to eliciting powerful emotional responses from the reader. Several scenes will stay with me long-term." ~ Amazon Customer

"The character development is superb." ~ Kindle Customer

"I feel as though Ben dared to allow readers to take a glimpse into his own soul and the issues that mattered to him. He did a superb job of bringing the characters to life in these pages and in invoking feeling from his readers." ~ Brittany

"I immediately jumped into the story and became so engaged I felt myself in the heroine's skin and within her aura." ~ Amazon Customer

"This was a compelling read that had me on the verge of tears. I felt so many different emotions while reading it."
~ Danielle Tara Evans

"I was pleasantly surprised by how willing I was to fall into his story. As far as the writing? Well, Starling clearly has a strong command of the written word. His use of dialogue is easy and natural. His ability to extract emotion is proficient (yes, I did cry)." ~ SR362

"If this is an example of everything Mr. Starling writes then I will read all he has to offer." ~ Roger Sprong

"I wasn't prepared for this novel. I had read short stories by Starling, so I knew it was going to have beautiful writing. However, I had no idea how he was going to weave together a story so seamlessly that it gave me chills. I know this will stay with me for a long time. " ~ Sarah

"I enjoyed this story from beginning to end, as author Ben Starling's writing evokes a myriad of emotions from joy to sadness and love to hate." ~ Sandra Jackson

"This is a well written, worthy book to read. If you are looking for a good book to read, no matter the genre, this is your book. You will enjoy it a lot." ~ Christy Bunch

"An excellent read! Enough plot to entertain an octopus…"
~ Amazon Customer

"A beautiful story, beautifully told. Ben Starling will be the author to watch, for he is surely going places…" ~ Jaye Marie

"This book was very nicely written. It is fast paced and has many plots and sub-plots. Mr. Starling's greatest asset is his ability to 'show, not tell.' The characters reveal their personalities and values through their own actions, and I found myself delighted at unusual perspectives, clever asides or astute titbits of information blended into the story line." ~ A Riley

"I loved the way the author, Ben Starling, describes everything in such revealing detail. I could smell the ocean and feel the sand between my toes. Everything came to life on the page and seemed so real." ~ Anita Dawes

"What a great book for relaxing. I really enjoy story line. Some very interesting twists and also shocking ending - you will never expected it :)" ~ Jitka Egressy

"Loved this book......kept me on edge... Beautifully written..... great suspense. Will try to find more books by this author." ~ Caroline Laughlin

"I feel as though Ben dared to allow readers to take a glimpse into his own soul and the issues that mattered to him. He did a superb job of bringing the characters to life in these pages and in invoking feeling from his readers. I look forward to reading more of his work..." ~ Brittany McCann

"Characterization is brilliant and, guaranteed, you won't be expecting the ending. Another wonderful story from author Ben Starling." ~ Diane White

"Captivated from page one, I read straight through to the end, amidst laughter, tears, palpitations, and heartache. I sighed with deep regret as I turned the last page, transfixed by a world I couldn't bear to leave..." ~ Mei-Mei Ellerman

"...this story was nothing short of a perfect thriller." ~ Shree

"Not once did Ben Starling tell me how to feel, he presented me with the actions and reactions of the characters and through those mini-stories within the story itself I formed my own dislike and distaste for certain characters and my love and admiration for others." ~ Cortney

"Ben Starling is a brilliant writer, and I look forward to reading more from him." ~ ESB

"If you are looking for a passionate story with characters who are both interesting and driven by the need to make a difference, you will not come away wanting…"
~ Margaret F.

"Though it is only a short story, Starling packs a lot in his well written plot." ~ Carole P. Roman

"Ben Starling has a gift of portraying strong emotion through his writing while also tying in a bigger picture of the threats society and the world pose on individuals."
~ Alysia Seymour

"It's heartbreakingly beautiful and is one of those stories that touches your soul and is deep on so many levels. Starling truly has a gift of appealing to the spiritual and emotional passions hidden within us all." ~ Jennifer L

"This story will make you laugh, dream, hope, cry, yearn, and tenderly hold your interest throughout…the story flowed, as does a superior novel, and the reader gets the feeling that there is all the time in the world and that he is, indeed, reading an unhurried novel with excellent character development. The author's words were chosen so carefully that the characters smoothly evolved into living, breathing, loving people with whom the reader could identify."
~ Phyllis Rader Eisenstadt

GOLDEN ROSE

PROLOGUE

My remaining time here is measured in hours. Were I invited to be more precise, I would hazard between three and four. Hence my urgency to complete this text, and share it with whomsoever should read it.

The document represents the development of journal notes that I recorded between 1897 and 1899. The notes remained under lock and key until now—June of 1914—when I have fleshed them out, added footnotes, etcetera.

Soon, I will be travelling to what it humours me to describe as *remote lands*, perhaps indefinitely.[1] As communication from those parts is notoriously problematic, my intention is to share an extraordinary story while introducing a theorem, a postulate, a dictum—call it what you will—that could prove as pertinent to the reader as to a soldier, sailor, tinker, tailor, or even, Prime Minister.[2]

Life's accelerating pace is evident at every turn. Consider the replacement of the horse-drawn hansom cab with the motorised automobile, or that abominable time-saver, the pre-tied bow tie. *Unde erit illud extremum?*[3] We now live our lives as if each minute might be our last. On account of the inevitable encroachment of sundry obligations upon the reader's leisure time, I am determined to capture the essence of this adventure with the minimum of ink. Cognisant that few will spare the time to read even an abridged prologue, I intend rewarding those who do, by sharing an excellent witticism I encountered in a music hall, this very week.

---

[1] How impoverished the language of Shelley, Keates, Tennyson, Shakespeare *et al* would be without euphemism!

[2] It will not have escaped your attention that I am an advocate of the Oxford comma. Soon enough, I trust the reason for my devotion to this superior grammatical utilisation will become evident.

[3] *Unde erit illud extremum?* Where will it all end?

As I reflect upon the events described herein, I am grateful for the loyalty of an old friend who has travelled with me these past years. If only Major Reginald "Raj" Dalton VC were here to share this moment, for it was he who set in motion the events culminating in a critical aspect of this narrative. While my fellow boarding school pupils were too entertained by his ramrod back, glass eye, and tales of derring-do (involving lands and cultures distant), to appreciate the wisdom he shared at the conclusion of his lessons, I found myself devouring every syllabub. Syllable. Without exception, he would open by referring to us as his *shining stars*—a title I am uncertain I, or any of us, deserved! Out of respect, I have elevated the very finest of his closing declarations to the status of a *Daltonism*.[4]

Major, I salute you and grasp this opportunity to repeat the sage words that comprise perhaps your most sagacious contribution: *humor plus aperit quam veritas*.[5]

I remain Sir, now and always, your most devoted and grateful pupil.

Robert Walters
June 29th, 1914

The sky that 1914 night veiled London beneath a sullen eiderdown of drizzle. The *staccato* clicking of steel-capped leather on cobble betrayed a man's rapid progress, as he sought out the shadows between the hissing gaslamps, in his efforts to remain unseen. The backstreet led to the servants' entrance of his grand townhouse, a mile distant. At this late hour, his furtive progress was unnecessary as the streets were

---

[4] The reader should not confuse my use of the word with the informal name for the medical condition protanopia, or colour blindness.

[5] *Humor plus aperit quam veritas*. Humour opens more doors than truth.

as empty as his conscience. Another evening spent in the arms of his brother's wife had brought a satisfaction matched only by the wealth he had accumulated following a series of shrewd underwriting bets in Lloyds of London.

He flipped the lid on an Asprey pocketwatch, a finger tracing the complex filigree engraving on its gold back. The time was well past midnight, which suited him as his staff would have retired to bed. His musings were replaced with a gasp when the darkness around him burst to life. Too late, he turned to ascertain the cause. Enveloped by a crazed assailant, he was driven to the ground. With one slash, the man's windpipe was severed, another opened his jugular. So brutal was the attack that he did not scream. He lay face-down in a pool of blood, undiscovered until the driver of the milk pram brought his horse to rest beside the corpse, five hours later.

Now let me share the promised witticism: *if William Penn's aunts owned a pastry shop, what price would they charge for their pies? Answer: the pie rates of Penn's Aunts.*[6] How that button-burster bruised my bellows—without doubt, it was the second most entertaining aspect of a long and eventful evening!

The body of this narration opens seventeen years previously—in 1897—at the auction house of Leonard Westerly & Nephew. My role, as observer rather than

---

[6] Permit me to mention that I am fortunate to have enjoyed no less than four performances of WS Gilbert and Arthur Sullivan's comic opera, *The Pirates of Penzance*, at the Savoy Theatre.

participant was predicated upon my status: I was a curious but impoverished student. The event involved an auction of curios and artefacts that had been considered incongruent with the contents of other sales. The selection had been assembled from every corner of the empire, and beyond.

Lot 28, currently being described by the auctioneer, originated from a remote, steamy and plague-riddled domain as yet unvisited by either Her Majesty's military or by His missionaries.

Attendance was somewhat sparse, explained no doubt by the fact that a number of objects offended the sensibilities of the God-fearing people of Buckingham, the highly respectable town in which the auction house had stood for a quarter of a century.

"...an excellent example of a shrunken head—attributed to one of the Jivaro peoples—probably the Shuar, whom experts agree are perhaps *the* most skilled practitioners of this barbaric craft. Your attention is drawn to the fine dermal toning—achieved via the digital application of liberal quantities of charcoal ash—and the object's excellent symmetry. Permit me to also draw your attention to its pronounced mandibular prognathism."

As I lamented the man's demonstrable inability to express himself in unornamented English, I beheld a grapefruit-sized object,[7] ebony in colour; as instructed, I permitted my attention to be drawn to its jutting jaw.

Without warning, a gentleman with a low centre of gravity and not inconsiderable altitude burst through the double doors at the rear of the room. His arrival garnered nudges and whispering. He assessed the assembled company through a monocle, before proceeding (with some awkwardness) along the central isle. His limp drew my gaze

---

[7] The shrunken head is markedly more compact than its animated progenitor on account of the shrinking process that involves several stages, including removing the skull, and boiling the head in a pot of water and herbs.

to his feet, which lacked the proportionate duplication expected of those extremities—indeed one trotter was nearly double the conventional size.

The unexpected did not terminate there: the cut of his tweed suit was double-breasted; the cross-stripe, a most sudden magenta. A beard that adopted the *Shenandoah Style*, cascaded down his front, resemblant of the Victoria Falls in full flood.

He thrust a black walking cane high into the air and shouted, "Good Sir, I pray my tardiness has not enabled lot 17—the Dobu Island fishing kite and associated paraphernalia—to escape my bidding."

The startled auctioneer answered, "Sir, I regret we have progressed to lot 28, the shrunken head."

"So the uKhandampevu Assegai—lot 21, if memory serves me—has also fallen beneath your gavel? That is most unfortunate as I was particularly drawn to that example, on account of the fact that it is recorded as having been prised from the chest of an unfortunate corporal of the Perthshire Light Infantry, following the Battle of Isandlwana. Whom, may I enquire, is the new owner?"

"In both cases, the successful bidder was the gentleman in the front row."

The recent arrival scrutinised the occupants of the aforementioned rank. He lingered upon one individual's posterior aspect.

"In which case, I shall bid a guinea for the shrunken head—in the hope that I may extract some small benefit from my visit—though I note the formidable competition this event has attracted."

"Thank you, Sir. We now have an opening bid from the gentleman standing."

This occasioned Mr Westerly's nephew, who had been observing the proceedings from the podium, to cough discreetly in order to attract the auctioneer's attention. The founder's relation then whispered into the broadcaster's ear which, along with his cheeks, adopted the identical shade of pink as his buttonhole carnation. The auctioneer bowed to the opening bidder.

Excuse me—we are most privileged to welcome you...*Your Grace.*"

The aristocrat's sparkling eyes resided in a head that displayed the weathered characteristics associated with excessive exposure to the extremes of climate. Despite his craggy appearance, a lady of indeterminate vintage appeared close to swooning, so vigorously did she fan her boat race.[8]

"You are most kind, Sir," he said, his smile warming the room.

A voice that I calculated originated from the front row— shouted, "Two guineas!"

I believe the opening bidder had recognised his rival as none other than Colonel Rhodes de Doublette-Fawltery (of the Derbyshire de Doublette-Fawlterys), a man who had steadfastly devoted his former career to the suppression of whichever native uprising threatened the re-election of Her Majesty's government.

Following the massacre of the gallant colonel's second regiment, it was inevitable he became encumbered with a nickname—and that it endured.

His retirement (and a not immodest portion of his not immodest inheritance) was committed to benefacting Oxford University's splendid Pitt Rivers museum—which vied, in my humble opinion, with that fine city's Ashmolean Museum for the title of most enjoyable location for student, visitor or professor, to disregard the passage of time. The curator of the Pitt Rivers, a man named Charles Simpson, was known to those of us whose interest lay in this field, to be actively expanding its shrunken head collection.

---

[8] I am not usually an advocate of Cockney rhyming slang (*boat race* = *face*). I make this exception, lest the reader has forgotten that in 1897, Oxford achieved an eighth consecutive victory against Cambridge in the 54th University Boat Race, extending their lead to 31–22. A lead that, I am entirely certain, will never be surrendered!

On each occasion that His Grace was outbid, he emitted a chuckle, and shouted *bravo*! And so it continued until the resolute colonel smelled victory at seven guineas, and sealed it with a final half-sovereign.

His Grace led the applause. His final words were, "Unfortunately, I have a pressing engagement involving a hyena and a taxidermist. Double-Fault's bottomless pockets have occasioned him a victory as splendid as that of Chard and Bromhead against the Zulu at Rorke's Drift. I congratulate you, Sir, on securing this item, and am indebted to you for my entertainment. With regret however, good people, I must take my leave. Good afternoon!"

The room exhaled. I turned to the gentleman beside me.

"Excuse me Sir, but who exactly was that most impressive gentleman?"

"That, young man, is the new owner of Montagu Hall— His Grace, the ninth Duke of Dingley."

"The sprawling and quite magnificent Baroque mansion in Northamptonshire?"

All two hundred rooms of it, but the word *magnificent* is redundant. Were that his fortune rivalled his charm! One can only speculate as to why he fritters away the estate's dwindling income in auction houses such as this, on curios such as that, when he cannot afford to repair the roof of a stately home compared with Blenheim and Castle Howard. These days it is little more than a repository for dusty portraits, ghoulish collectibles and stuffed animals."

At this moment I noticed that the formerly-swooning lady had anchored close by, and appeared to be listening to our conversation.

I said, "I've read of that family and recall that their fortune came from the slave trade and sugar plantations of the *mundus novus*."[9]

The man answered, "You are well informed, young man.

---

[9] *Mundus novus*. New world.

But most of it has been dissipated in the *old world* by a succession of increasingly profligate dukes."

The lady now shook her head and *tut-tutted* with sufficient ardour that the gentlemen was obliged to pause, regard her, and collect himself before continuing.

"And their woes increase: recently, in addition to the crumbling hall, the tenant farmers report mutilated livestock. Many have abandoned their tenancies. Rumours abound that a madman prowls the woods, emerging at night to butcher sheep. First the constabulary, and now the keepers—who set man-traps—have failed to apprehend the blood-crazed villain. In fact—"

The lady advanced. "Sir, there will always be those who have nothing better to do than spread mischief by criticising the good, the mighty, the *magnificent*."

"Madam, I only wished to inform—"

"Poppycock, Sir! You should be deeply ashamed of yourself!"

With that broadside, she set sail.

Twenty-six months later, in June of 1899, the final Examination of my Bachelor's degree in Anthropology at Oxford University was successfully completed with First Class Honours.

I had now committed myself to a doctorate in that fine discipline, though the subject of my thesis persisted in eluding me. In the hope of identifying a particular aspect of research, and in order to provide some income, I had taken temporary employment in the basement of the city's Ashmolean Museum. My duties included verifying the provenance of the more obscure objects, some of which had been donated by Elias Ashmole himself, in 1677. I had just confirmed that the Crondall Hoard of gold coin contained seventy-three examples of Anglo-Saxon *thrymsa*, and twenty-four of Merovingian origin, when I received a message requesting my presence in the senior curator's office, post-haste.

The sun glinted upon Dr Ambrose Parson's bald pate. The room was disorderly—so much so, that I wondered how he had organised his thoughts and writings sufficiently to be awarded a doctorate in 1863, with a thesis titled: *Ritual Slaughter and the Importance of Profuse Bloodletting from the Ears and Tongue in Mayan Worship.*[10]

He looked up from his desk, raising a jungly eyebrow for emphasis, and smiled. "Well done, lad. Impeccable attention to detail, once again. I knew were the right fellow for the job."

"Sir?"

"Which is why I requested your presence. We've been approached by a prominent collector who is in need of a conscientious individual to catalogue his, shall I say, *eclectic* collection? He's somewhat local—his vast estate lies in Northamptonshire—"

"Would that be the Duke of Dingley?"

"Ah—a man whose reputation, as they say, precedes him. I recommended you, and I am prepared to allow you a week's unpaid leave to complete the task. But I'm afraid there's a catch…"

"That he refuses to imburse me for my services?"

---

[10] No doubt the fascinating choice of subject helped.

The eyebrow climbed higher. "As I said, his reputation precedes him. Despite my efforts to negotiate on your behalf, His Grace was adamant that free transport there and back, a most comfortable room, first class dining, fine wine with your evening meal, and ale at luncheon, represent more than adequate compensation. Perhaps something in his collection might nudge you towards the subject of your doctorate, as the closing date for your decision grows ever closer."

"After considerable thought, I have reduced the field to two possible subjects. I am as fascinated by a Nilotic people in the southern Sudan whose culture, I understand, revolves entirely around their cattle...as I am in holding a Dixey magnifying glass to the role of the gift amongst those North-West Coast Indians that practice the *Potlatch* ceremony. I have often considered the consequences of the 1884 Indian Act upon the culture, society and economy of the Haida, Tlingit, Nootka, Salish—"

"If I may interject? Both are most worthy avenues of scholarship. I suggest you do not dally, lad. In my opinion, it is only a matter of time before other academics alight upon these areas of enquiry, which might—"

"Damage my chances of securing a lectureship at the university? You are, of course, correct, Sir. The field is becoming increasingly congested, so it appears that I have little to lose in accepting this assignment—other than a roof over my head—as my rent, like my thesis topic, is in danger of evolving from due to overdue."

"Permit me to impress upon you an opinion I have developed quite recently: the academic world in general and our subject in particular should strive to shine a light upon some aspect of the human condition, lest one day we awake to find ourselves irrelevant. From irrelevance flows the very real danger that our fine subject, and in time perhaps the glorious university itself, will crumble to dust."

"You are suggesting that in terms of John Venn's diagram of interlocking circles, there needs to be significant overlap between our anthropological contributions and the goings-on in the life of the man on the Clapham omnibus?"

"Indeed so. I am reminded that I have a quite fascinating thesis upon my bookshelf that codifies the contrapuntal improvisation contained in Aka-Baka pygmy music—I have enjoyed rereading it almost annually since its submission—but the question is, what societal function does this work provide?"

"Might I borrow your copy?"

After nodding, he said, "I refer to the presentation of an original body of work as the *Alpha Objective*. By delivering scholarship that makes a societal contribution, you will be satisfying what I refer to as the oft-disregarded *Beta Objective*."

"This terminology is new to me."

"To be of lasting value, a thesis should also have relevance a hundred years hence. I call this the *Gamma Objective*."

"Of course, it will be the responsibility of those who come after us to judge whether the third objective has been satisfied," I added.

"Indeed so. And don't for one instant underestimate the temporal and cerebral commitment required to satisfy the examiners."

"I am under no such illusion."

"Good, because your premise will need to be as succulent as a Peach Melba, as insightful as *The Mikado*, and as unsinkable as HMS Hero.[11] Remember that once you have written it, you must polish it for months before even considering submission. As my tutor, Professor Magnus Berkeley—God rest his soul—used to say, nothing good is

---

[11] Which sank in the North Sea in 1908. It further warrants recording that the mighty ironclad battleship's primary weapon was an armoured prow for the purpose of ramming its enemies. Naval historians are universal in their conclusion that it was the most useless battleship ever launched.

ever written or re-written—only re-re-written."[12]

"I understand that the professors will employ a speculum to prize apart the hemispheres of my brain to examine its contents. However, I am ready for the challenge. But, with respect, you omitted to mention one of the examiners' strictest criteria: in the event that I include another's scholarship, it must be unambiguously attributed."

"Sir, we are both Oxford men—hence I considered mentioning *plagiarism* (he spat the word out with the violence with which one would eject a rancid oyster) entirely unnecessary. Returning to the life of an academic, you are no doubt aware that the financial rewards are meagre."

"I am resigned to a life of impoverishment, as my other passion also offers little prospect of financial reward."

"You are considering entering the Church?"

"Such a career remains an option, of course. But I was in fact considering an alternative which I am uncomfortable sharing with you, in case you laugh not with, but *at* me."

"I shall do no such thing."

"Very well. Like all men, I have my imaginings. Since my youngest days, I have been drawn to the sea and the great fighting ships that do battle upon it. But this interest is trifling when compared with my fascination for the world *beneath* the waves. I dream of building an underwater vessel that combines the finest design elements of Garrett's second *Resurgam*, Monturiol's *Ictineo 2*, and Borgeois and Brun's *Le*

---

[12] Dr Parsons' presumption that his former tutor, Magnus "Bonkers" Berkeley is no longer with us, is evidentially inhibited but logically sound. In '78, the Professor Emeritus sailed aboard his yacht *Callisto* to within a mile of North Sentinel Island in the Bay of Bengal. The yacht's captain stated at the inquiry that Professor Berkeley then paddled a canoe, laden with linen tablecloth, fine silverware and a Fortnum & Mason hamper, towards the rocky shoreline. His intention was recorded as *an unquenchable desire to introduce the natives to that essential institution, the English luncheon.* The inquiry concluded that it was not only the foie gras that were consumed with relish.

Plongeur."

Dr Parsons' mouth had fallen open. In my desire to convince him of the merits of my ambitions, I continued.

"My vessel will remain submerged for days at a time, and will be capable of diving far *below the thunders of the upper deep* in order that the passengers might observe the *huge sea worms* and *enormous polypi* that *winnow with giant arms the slumbering green.* There you have it—my indulgence is to discover the *Kraken!*"[13]

"I would suggest your indulgence is better described as to *discover death by drowning.* Now, if you will forgive my change of tack, I feel beholden to mention that following the tragedy..."

Dr Parsons' tone lowered in unison with the obedient eyebrow.

"...it was in the newspapers. His Grace took a wife some eighteen months ago. To this day, the exceedingly lavish nuptials remain the talk of society. Many hundreds of guests attended an event that was calculated by the editor of *The Illustrated London News* to have cost at least £18,850![14]

"She was a great beauty three decades his junior, whose family had amassed a fortune from the steel mills that supply the shipbuilding and railway industries. Those lucky enough to encounter her confirmed the appropriateness of her sobriquet, *Golden Rose,* on account of her Christian name, and honey-coloured locks that turned to gold in sunlight. She was also well loved for her great intelligent, and compassion."

"*Was?*"

"The South American continent was chosen for an extended honeymoon. A considerable portion of time was spent in the hostile jungles of Amazonia, in order that the

---

[13] Mindful of the recent discussion of authorial attribution, I confirm that the italicised language is not mine, but that of Alfred, Lord Tennyson (1809-1892).

[14] As prices never cease rising, I calculate that that sum would equate to no less than £20,252 today!

duke might complete his collection."

"Does a collector ever truly *complete* a collection?"

"I understand that His Grace sought one final object before he intended devoting his efforts to display, experimentation and scholarship. What that object was, I do not know. What I *do* know is that catastrophe struck...perhaps you'd rather...?"

"I can handle it, Sir."

"Very well. It's as if I read the account this very morning on the front page of *The Banbury Bugle*, so vividly do I recall the frightful details. One evening the duchess was capturing a vivid sunset with watercolours—which the reporter stated was her passion—when she was seized by a jaguar. Her wounds were fearful—she was mauled extensively and a leg was torn off. By the time the duke had put a bullet through the beast's heart, it was too late. She returned with him nine months ago in a coffin, and was buried, following a most private ceremony, in the mausoleum adjoining the estate chapel."

"I encountered the duke some time ago. This whole affair must have affected him dreadfully..."

"And *you* lad? How are *you*, these days? No one should have to go through what you—"

"It's been two years now. I am coping, Sir."

"I am relieved to hear it."

After a quarter-minute during which we stared at the others' shoes, Dr Parsons cleared his throat, and resumed communicating.

"Like you, the duke studied anthropology at the university. But his thesis was rejected on account of insufficient verisimilitude and excessive imaginings. His tutor, the eminent Professor Sir Rufus Reynolds—may he also rest in peace—reported to me that what the duke presented to the examiners bordered on the delusional."

Another lengthy pause drove the point home.

"Reynolds also informed me that this considerable academic setback did nothing to diminish the young man's love of life, though the good professor lamented the waste of a brilliant mind."

"Surely the thesis was adjusted and resubmitted?"

"Of course he was invited to do so. Instead, he vanished for the best part of three decades, apparently living with natives in Africa, the Americas and Pacific islands, where he collected items and conducted research obsessively, no doubt to prove the veracity of his absurd ideas. Shortly after his return to England in '95—before he had assumed the dukedom—his cousin, the eighth duke, met a gruesome end. Consequently, the title passed to the present duke entirely unexpectedly, and he moved into the great house shortly thereafter.

"And before you ask, the current duke's unfortunate predecessor was discovered in his grounds one morning in a shocking state. His femoral artery had been severed and other deep wounds lacerated his neck and head. His face was locked in a grimace of exquisite terror. The coroner recorded a verdict of murder and concluded that two weapons had been employed in the attack: a sharp blade had severed the artery and an instrument of unknown origin had caused the gouging. In the hope of identifying the assassin, enquiries were conducted regarding escaped inmates from lunatic asylums proximate and distant. This proved an infertile avenue of enquiry."

"Do you have any thoughts on this most unsettling matter?"

"None worth sharing."

Dr Parsons opened the drawer of his desk and retrieved a Bible.

"The Reverend Carter was here yesterday—dropped off half a dozen copies for me to distribute, as he is wont to do. By the way, he mentioned he hadn't seen you in church recently."

"It's true that other matters have—"

"It is of no concern to me, but I'd suggest you lock your door each evening. He asked me to encourage you to dip into The Good Book before bed."

"Considering the potential for danger that you have introduced into this assignment, I will consider doing so."

"Let me add that we are all impressed how you have not let your family tragedy deflect you."

"I am an Englishman, Sir."

"Garnet Wolseley himself would be proud of you, lad. Upon the shoulders of men like you, this great empire was built. If I may make a suggestion? Have you considered taking a wife? I'm certain the right woman would bring joy back into your life. Why not settle down…start a family?"

"Sadly, I fear that my perfect woman exists only in my dreams."

"Fair enough. Now, back to the business in hand. I suggest you don't stroll outdoors after dark; and avoid the woods at all times. If I were you, I'd lock your door at night and leave the key in place. The madman may still be concealing himself about those environs."

"If I may return to a previous topic, did Professor Reynolds have more to say on the subject of the thesis?"

"He was a man who rarely employed hyperbole. However, we were due to meet to discuss a matter he had described as *extraordinarily disturbing*, but tragically, he was run down by the number eleven tram on his way back from the British Museum, where he'd been conducting research that he described as *anthropologically obscure*. All I know is that his research was in some way connected with the rejected thesis."

Dr Parsons had detected my growing reservations regarding the prospective enterprise.

"You'll be fine, lad. As one of my many failings is incessant curiosity, I'll tell you what I'm prepared to do for you. The assignment's duration is one week. Return with information that sheds light upon this catalogue of mysteries, and I'll pay you ten shillings from my own pocket."

"That is *most* generous, Sir!"

"Another thing—I know that the application of scissors

to that wayward mane is anathema to you—but you simply cannot meet the duke in that state! Here's a half crown. Go to that excellent barber in The Turl—ask for McKenzie—and get a decent haircut!"

I decided it was politic to agree. "Yes, of course."

"Now, I discussed this matter with Mrs Parsons. Her advice was that you should find an ally at Montagu hall—someone other than the duke—who might provide information. Of course she was at pains to stress that the duke is known to be a man without stain..." He smiled.

I decided it was politic to smile.

"Finally, if all else fails, Mrs P is an advocate of arousing your subject's anger, because fury deprives a man of caution. Her exact words were: *it's not only pride that comes before a fall.*"

I decided it was politic to be politic.

"I will follow this excellent advice, Dr Parsons."

SUNDAY– *note to self: how fortunate that an unexpected opportunity has arisen that I will grasp with both hands. Let the adventure begin!*

I am no expert on sheep. Consequently, I am unaware if the appetite of one breed may dwarf that of another; or if a grass that tastes sweet to a highland ram may induce gagging in its lowland counterpart. Could this ovine phenomenon be analogous to the antipodal response people have to my favourite member of the cabbage family—the sweet and succulent Brussels sprout? I mention this gap in my education because the sheep scattered throughout the parkland in which Montagu Hall was set were, for whatever reason, negligent in their duty of trimming the grass.

Upon reflection, I concede that this may have been explained with reference to their meagre numbers, which itself may have been explained with reference to the dwindling number of tenant farmers, which itself may have been explained with reference to the mutilated livestock. The crows, by contrast, had multiplied to such an extent that their presence could be observed at every point of the compass. Clusters of them hopped and stared, as these birds are inclined to do.

The elms that lined the drive were impressive, but the weeds poking through the gravel, spied through the window of my hansom, contributed to the estate's unkempt air; as did the moss-covered boughs that littered the vista. The cornflower blue of the sky reflected most pleasingly in a sizeable lake, the boundaries of which were obscured by weeping willows. Beyond the water, thick woodland stained the panorama that extended to the horizon.

During the journey, I had occupied myself reflecting upon the due date of my rent and the combined counsel of Dr and Mrs Parsons. I felt disappointment that the vast fountain the drive swelled to accommodate—comprising buxom maidens rising from giant clam shells—was reduced to no more than a trickle; and why had a groundsman failed to remove the dove that floated in that stagnant concavity?

My disappointment gave way to curiosity when I noticed a young woman perched upon the edge of the fountain. Her stillness was absolute. The straw hat that concealed her features prevented me determining whether she was aware of our arrival...but the unexpected lightness of mind that settled upon me evinced that she was exceedingly fair. In any event, she did not raise her head to acknowledge us, so my smile went unreturned.

A scruffy dog—its appearance suggested a Border Terrier-haystack mix—tugged at her ankle. Its efforts to gain the woman's attention proved in vain, so absorbed was she by her thoughts.

The hall itself, comprising a central block and wings, was Baroque in design and of vast dimensions. The mellowed limestone, where staining was not evident, gave a most pleasing appearance. Typical of Vanbrugh's flamboyance, I spied coronets, urns and cherubs upon the roof that attempted to draw the eye away from the imposing chimneys. The façade was generously decorated with Doric pilasters and the occasional cypher. The windows, which were numerous and large, were mostly shuttered.

The front door—that towered above me—was of oak construction, freckled with iron studs. The quantity of timber employed was sufficient to have built a second Cutty Sark. The door rested in shadow behind the Corinthian columns of an imposing portico, above which the stonework adopted an indented aspect. This indentation housed a life-sized statue of an individual and my immediate reaction was poetic: *whose frown and wrinkled lip, and sneer of cold command...*[15] Higher still, the Union Flag hung limply in the afternoon air. It was set at half-mast, no doubt, out of respect for the recent misfortune that had befallen this pre-eminent family.

The oak doors eased open and I was greeted by a mountainous footman with the face of a prizefighter who had won few prizes. Though the man bore scant resemblance to Bob Fitzsimmons,[16] it suits me to employ the latter's patronym when recording the former's contribution to this narrative.

"'Is Grace'll be with ya in doo corse, Suh,"[17] Fitz announced with a bow as he closed the doors to the musty room in which he left me.

The chair I occupied was positioned at the ocular

---

[15] *...tell that its sculptor well those passions read which yet survive; stamped on these lifeless things, the hand that mocked them, and the heart that fed...* from *Ozymandias*, by Percy Bysshe Shelley (1792-1822). I invite the reader to consider, in the light of this second attribution, my sensitivity toward even the most oblique accusation of plagiarism.

[16] The Cornish boxer who won the World Heavyweight Championship in '97.

[17] For readers unfamiliar with the Northamptonshire working class accent, I have in this example substituted *Sir* with *Suh*. Elsewhere, I have made adjustments that I trust capture this *fudged vowel* dialect.

epicentre of the legion of portraits that hung on panelled walls. The duke's male ancestors stood stiffly in military attire, reclined in ermine, or sat resplendent in hunting pink upon nostril-flaring stallions. Hair piled high, their female counterparts wore billowy dresses and clasped fluffy Spaniels.[18] Two thoughts immediately occurred to me. The second was that they all—relative and pet—stared at me.

The unmistakable profile of the duke passed some distance from the window. I watched him limp towards a greenhouse into which he disappeared.

Time passed. Weighty Footsteps then alerted me to an imminent arrival, and the door swung open. His Grace entered.

He was much as I remembered: the beard plunged towards a stomach that continued to demonstrate its owner's contempt for that current fad, the tapeworm diet.[19] The tweeds hovered midway between rust and ochre. The cloth was dissected by vertical stripes of crimson; canary yellow equivalents performed the horizontal function.[20]

He eyed me up and down. "My dear fellow—you must be Walters."

"At you service, Your Grace."

"Sincere apologies if you've been waiting long."

I was about to engage him in small-talk regarding his apparent interest in plants, but he was speaking again.

"So much for modern technology—the two-twenty from Paddington lost steam. Set foot here five minutes ago."

---

[18] Which reminds me of the man who bought a dog from a locksmith. When he got home, it made a bolt for the door.

[19] Which was a welcome culinary omen!

[20] Tweeds are designed for Scottish estates so that the keepers, stalkers and ghillies blend with the landscape. A kindly kilted Celt at Campbell's of Beauly once informed me that drabber grey tweeds are preferred on the rockier estates of western Scotland, while browns are associated with the grouse moors to the east. Perhaps His Grace had ordered this particular tweed in order that he might remain undetected in the vibrant jungles of Amazonia.

"My time has been profitably employed studying the many fine portraits of your impressive ancestors."[21]

He poured himself a drink. "Care for a whisky?"

"No thank you, Your Grace. It's not to my taste."

"I didn't much care for it at your age either. Something one grows into. Now tell me something about your family."

"My father was a country vicar. He always hoped I would follow his calling. My mother was known locally for her art. She specialised in horse portraiture—especially of the rarer breeds."

"A latter-day Stubbs, eh? I think we've got a few of his works hanging about the place—I really should catalogue my art collection too. I noticed you referred to both parents in the past tense. None of my business, of course, but…"

"I appreciate that, Your Grace."

"Fair enough. Now that splendid man Parsons informs me you're a methodical and reliable fellow, intent on embarking upon a doctorate. He claims that you have been passionate about native cultures for some considerable time."

"My mother claims that my first spoken word was *aboriginal*."

He laughed.

"There is hardly a museum I haven't visited or a book I haven't read on the subject, Your Grace."

"Excellent! Do share with me where your interests lie."

He moved to the window, his swollen foot clumping beside him. With each impact, a puff of dust erupted from the threadbare carpet.

"I am presently undecided but hope that the week I spend cataloguing your magnificent collection might spark my interest in an obscure but suitable scholarly niche, upon which to focus my efforts. My task is made no easier by Dr

---

[21] The first thought generated by the portraits was that the duke's family was populated with uncommonly unhandsome specimens.

Parsons suggesting I select a topic that sheds light upon an aspect of the human condition."

"Stuff and nonsense! It is sufficient that your topic interest you, and you alone!"

The black walking stick upon which he relied for balance was striking—perhaps it was the one he had waved in the auction house. I could see that a craftsman of uncommon adroitness had fashioned a skull mid-shaft; entwined snakes occupied the upper portion; one cobra head, which was set at the perpendicular, functioned as a handle. The object was almost certainly mahogany, probably the work of a member of the Nguni people of southern Africa.

Staring at the outside world, the duke said, "It took me four years to settle upon my subject—but once I had, never for a moment did I regret it. Beware though that the esteemed professors who will evaluate your academic contribution won't be looking for anything daring or original."

He turned to face me.

"In order that I may better understand your intellectual orientation, where do you stand in relation to the work of Darwin?"

"While not my field of study, I find myself at times somewhat persuaded by his thesis, Your Grace. At other times…"[22]

"Tell me what you know of Burton and Hunt."

"The founders of the Anthropological Society of London which was set up in opposition to the same city's Ethnological Society? The gentlemen brought to the fore the debate between monogenism and polygenism."[23]

"Now think carefully before you answer. Which do you find the more compelling?"

I was faced with an equal prospect of upsetting the duke

---

[22] This left me sufficient room to adjust my position, should the duke indicate that he possessed strong views on the subject.

[23] Doubtless, you will agree that both possess merits and demerits.

within minutes of our meeting. I needed to think quickly. And well.

"I am grateful for your enquiry, Your Grace, because I have considered this matter frequently. I am resolutely committed to what is, without doubt, the more compelling paradigm."[24]

"Yes, yes—tell me! Which one?"

"The *monopoly-genism* school."

"The *what?* I don't think I've heard of—" He eyed me thoughtfully, then, chest heaving, boomed with laughter.

"Excellent answer! Top drawer, young man! Tell me, have they assigned you some young, enthusiastic tutor?"

"A man named Dr Robson Riley-Roper. An authority on—"

"Can't say I recognise the name, but does he get out into the field? Has he *gone native,* or is he one of those arm-chair academics whose best work is done in the Senior Common Room over middling port and Junior cigars?"

"His doctorate addressed the economic impact of the slave trade in Africa and The United States. He has travelled extensively in both. A book on the subject followed. I can confirm that its content is interesting, well argued, and the photographs further support his thesis that the activity benefitted every American citizen to the princely sum of eleven dollars and sixty cents *per annum.*"

"Sounds like the a man I should invite to supper…"

He smiled and I mirrored his expression.

"Let us lose no more time—I will introduce you to my modest collection. Something tells me you'll enjoy it…"

---

[24] This answer (and the duke's evaluation of it) procured me a further eighteen seconds.

Three expansive rooms in the east wing housed the Americas, Pacific Islands and Africa collections. They smelled of Terezol furniture polish and fresh paint. The large-windowed chambers, glossy walls and glass-fronted cabinets contributed to an ambience that contrasted with the stuffy corridors we had negotiated earlier.

The duke introduced me to the Pacific Islands collection first. The display cabinets were populated with clothing decorated with shell, elaborate costumes and grotesque death masks, brutal cannibal tools, clubs, and other curios too numerous to mention. I cannot control myself: creatures of ocean and land occupied sealed glass containers that ranged in size from pickling jars to ale barrels; the liquid they bathed in shared the coppery tint of the flying fox's head. This is my last word on the subject: a collection of this calibre would not have played second fiddle to the British Museum…and there were two additional rooms!

"You need not concern yourself with the flora and fauna—a man named Perkins from the Natural History Museum is due next week. But I see your gaze has fixed upon Osbert, my preserved octopus. You'll agree those iridescent rings—though a little faded—give him a unique appearance. Notice how modestly his size compares with the creature our Gallic neighbours call *poulpe*, and insist on submerging beneath an entire Mediterranean of garlic butter. Unlike its edible cousin, should my blue-ringed friend bite you, you can expect to vomit, suffer paralysis, blindness, respiratory and heart failure. I have timed the interlude between bite and death at a trifle under thirteen minutes for an adult and nine for a child. Incidentally, the Tulagian girl who thrust her hand into my Hardy fishing creel believed— for reasons I cannot possibly explain—that it contained liquorice toffees. Her last words—and I paraphrase—were that the bite was less significant than that of a mosquito."

"Thirteen and nine minutes? Your scientific rigour is impressive, Your Grace."

"Which compares with the death I chronicled of a Bantu

warrior, following envenomation by Africa's most deadly serpent, the black mamba. The less well known symptoms that I recorded included ptosis, bulbar palsy, paresthesia, dysarthria, fasciculations, and ataxia, before respiratory failure and cardiovascular collapse, caused death. The whole episode took from midway through breakfast—oh, how the infuriating Asa insisted on always overcooking my guineafowl eggs—until I had finished my third post-prandial cognac."

"I remain in awe of you attention to detail, Your Grace."

His eyes focused upon an idea. "I have often wondered whether this octopus venom might be manufactured in the laboratory. For medicinal purposes, you understand?"

"I understand, Your Grace."

"Excellent fellow! I see we will get on famously."

As he introduced me to objects, he would test me by pointing with his walking stick and asking, "And what do you suppose that is?"

"A Fijian fishing trap—usually positioned alongside mangroves to capture fish on the falling tide."

He smiled. "I see I've employed the right man for the job."

The Africa Room contained a similarly varied and impressive collection of artefacts, preserved plants, and stuffed animals. Regarding the latter, there were examples of lion, cheetah, leopard, hyena, and jackal—all predators, I noted. An axe—probably a *Nzappa zap* of Congo origin—protruded from between the glass eyes of a gargantuan stuffed crocodile.

"The villagers believe that creature had killed as many as ninety men, women and children. However, what can they expect if they insist on fishing and washing in the river…"

The jaws of a gin trap gripped a wild dog's ankle.

"They are highly social animals," the duke said. "The entire pack had surrounded that male. One had broken several teeth chewing on the iron in its attempts to release its brother."

He stopped beside a cabinet that contained a bundle of dried leaves. An illustration captured the living plant. Spotted with orange fruit, it was generally unexceptional in appearance.

"I'll bet the Natural History fellow—what was his name again?"

"Perkins, I believe," I offered.

"Ah yes, Perkins. I bet he has no idea of the extraordinary magical power contained in the root bark of that divine plant, *Tabernanthe iboga*."

I repeated *Tabernanthe iboga* several times to myself to ensure the name was lodged in my memory, before speaking. "It looks wholly innocuous. Could you afford me a description of its magic, Your Grace?"

The duke's eyes lost focus. "Those who partake of it report of journeying to a place of beautiful, vivid colours unknown within our spectrum—imagine a blazing rainbow of infinite variety where the normal rules of hue, value and chroma are discarded in favour of something infinitely more magnificent. A dreamlike phase follows, in which you may encounter the most terrifying fiends and demons, before embarking upon a journey of deep introspection…"

When finally he rejoined me, he said, "Forgive me. No words can possibly do justice to its power and it was presumptuous of me to attempt to do so."

"Nonetheless, I appreciate your description of this fascinating plant."

I then successfully identified a Nagu fetish used in Vodun magic but shortly thereafter, I suggested a carved figurine was elephant tusk.

"So Walters, you are fallible! It's rhinoceros horn!" he laughed. "Now you are putting ideas in my head. Perhaps I should get word to Parsons that I will fine him a half crown for every error in your cataloguing!"

"But I would never forgive myself for bankrupting the unfortunate Dr Parsons, Your Grace."

The duke was humming a cheery tune as we entered the

Americas Room, my initial perusal of which indicated that the collection was biased towards the southern continent. However, clothing, pipes, pottery and the tools of hunting and warfare—much of it of Lakota, Menominee and Cree origin—were on display. A finely carved bear totem scraped the ceiling in one corner of the room. Other totemic animals, including coyote, wolf, and eagle held station elsewhere.

The major part of the room however, did contain objects originating in South America. Two displays caught my eye, but before I approached them, I beheld a panoply of blowpipes, darts, war bonnets, rattles and bows. It was at an elaborately decorated drum that I next directed my gaze.

"Impressive, isn't it?" the duke asked.

"As is the entire collection. I see here fine headdresses, ear-danglers and necklaces that had escaped my attention. I look forward to cataloguing each and every item."

His Grace observed me keenly via the monocle he had employed, as I approached the two objects that had first garnered my attention.

The first was a great stuffed bird. Its plumage was largely black, though a white collar encircled its neck and that same shade spilled onto the folded wings. The head was repulsive and featherless, with the sagging skin you might expect on shaving the head of an obese bulldog. A flap of limp flesh performed poorly the function of a crest; the snout finished with the cruelly hooked beak of a raptor. The feet were, even in this lifeless specimen, unsettling, terminating with claws that passed for facsimiles of the fearsome *shamshir*.[25]

---

[25] *Shamshir* is a Persian word that means *curved like a lion's claw*—a name shared by a long-bladed sword. Major Dalton often recounted how a private's arm was severed with a single blow from this formidable weapon, before he discharged his .442 calibre Beaumont–Adams revolver into the tribesman's chest. The major's platoon was surrounded by hundreds of insurgents, with reinforcements days away. Wounded, exhausted, hungry, low on ammunition, somehow the major—perhaps this account is best left for another occasion.

This creature dwarfed the African vultures with which I assumed it shared remote kinship. But it was the linen binding that covered the bird's eyes that required explanation. When I directed an enquiring expression at the duke, it went ignored.

"The mighty Andean Condor. The zoologist will insist that at eleven feet and four inches, it possesses the largest wingspan of any bird and that it can live to fifty years of age." Stroking the creature's shoulder in a gesture of fondness, he added, "*Fifty years?* What do mere zoologists know?" He turned to me, gripped my eyes with his, and asked, "What do you think of when observe such a magnificent creature?"

"Are you alluding to our previous conversation...of concepts such as random mutation and natural selection?"[26]

"All well and good, I suppose. But I'll share with you what I think of. I think of flight. Soaring on outstretched wings above mountain, valley, cloud forest. Letting the gusts and thermals take me where they will. That's what occupies my mind; not that confounded Darwin fellow everyone feels compelled to discuss all the time. Do you understand?"

I have previously recorded my craving to explore beneath the waves, but now seemed an inopportune juncture at which to complicate the discussion.

"I too have such imaginings, almost daily, Your Grace! Surely to dream of flight is a sign of a powerful imagination? A sign that you aren't prepared to be tethered to the conventional, the boring, the accepted norms of life."

"I am enjoying what I hear. Do continue."

The duke's interjection had given me an opportunity to refine my thoughts.

"How have we British made our greatest advances—be they Savery's steam engine, Jenner's vaccination for smallpox, Faraday's harnessing of electricity? By, of course,

---

[26] You will agree that this answer cunningly bought me time to sit on the fence.

first *dreaming* of a better world!"

"Excellent fellow—I see that we have more in common than I anticipated." He laughed. "But, correct me if I'm mistaken—do I detect that you have a question for *me*?"

"I was wondering…what object will be displayed *here*?"

I indicated the second object that had caught my attention: a glass-sided, brass-framed container, perhaps twenty-four inches tall and eight across. Raised on a plinth, it occupied pride of place in the centre of the room, and stood empty.

"Patience, my dear fellow. I received word today that this unique collectible will be delivered shortly. I will provide its catalogue entry myself. Now, lest I forget…"

He opened one of the taller windows in the room, justifying his action thus: "A little air circulation discourages the formation of mould on these sultry nights."

"A wise precaution, Your Grace, as we all know the devastation mould can wreak upon items unaccustomed to our climate."

Leaving the collection behind, we proceeded along a corridor as His Grace slid the key with which he had locked the door, into his breast pocket. "You will catalogue using graphite pencil, during the hours of nine to five. I will check your entries immediately thereafter. No need to ink them—I have a calligrapher in mind who will perform that duty when I have verified their accuracy. For security reasons, I prefer to keep the wing locked from six-thirty, at the latest. I'll have you shown to your room, and your evening meal sent up to you at seven-thirty. Forgive me if I don't join you, but I'm not much of a night bird."

Apparently, some humour resided in this final statement, causing him to laugh vigorously. On regarding my perplexed expression, he added, "A personal joke, you understand?"

Before I could answer, he nodded goodbye and left me standing there. I do not know whether the words he spoke when he was out of sight were intended for my ears: "Finally, yes *finally*, the collection will be complete."

My valise unpacked, I sat upon the bed, with my journal and Dr Parsons' Bible resting on the adjacent table. I confess that the proximity of the latter afforded me some comfort. The evening sky was observable through a generous gap where the undersized (and tatty) curtains failed to marry. The room, like the remainder of the house displayed no evidence of recent investment. I corrected myself: the décor of the portion of the east wing that housed the collection two floors below, was bright and shiny.

I anticipated encountering few obstacles in the production of an accurate catalogue. As for the duke himself: larger than life. Charming. And possessed of a contagious passion for the greatest subject in the world.

I *did* detect a mistruth regarding his explanation for keeping me waiting, but that moved me no closer to the ten shillings. However, perhaps I was being unreasonable. Was it not possible that he had returned on the train, wandered into the greenhouse, and like all avid horticulturalists, lost track of time as he administered to his beloved plants? The day, however, had been long and not without entertainment. Tomorrow I would commence work in earnest.

A knock on my door interrupted my reverie. Upon opening it, I found a tray outside. I dined on cold mutton stew, and drank a large glass of quarrelsome Burgundy. The stilton lacked creaminess, the slice of Shrewsbury cake was stale.[27]

Clearly, the day had drained more from me that I had realised. I was in bed at nine, and that was when I

---

[27] My immediate reaction was disappointment, but then I realised it was Sunday night, and no doubt the kitchen staff's duties were reduced substantially at the end of the weekend.

experienced my second disappointment: the mattress felt as if the horsehair had been replaced with coconuts.

Over the next hour, I writhed and turned in my efforts to achieve a degree of comfort. I endeavoured to think of matters other than to which part of my body my blood no longer flowed.[28] Eventually I lay still, willing sleep to overwhelm me.

MONDAY – *note to self: with my catalogue duties commencing, I must not allow them to absorb me so entirely that I forget my other mission.*

I was woken around seven by the call of crows. I rose cautiously, stretching my limbs to encourage the blood to flow back into my muscles. Satisfied that the mattress had not crippled me, I dressed, while reflecting upon the fact that I remembered no dreams, which was unusual, as I can be active in that department. Indeed, uncommon is the night in which I escape the embrace of Morpheus.[29] What I did recall was a sound of tapping on the roof above my room that occurred as the moon approached its culmination.

My poor recollection of the duration of this disturbance was, like my thick head, no doubt a casualty of the wine. What I did recall, despite being trapped in a half-sleep, was a

---

[28] Such as the name of that plant, *Tabernanthe iboga.*

[29] In the unlikely event that the reader has been denied a classical education, I can confirm that Morpheus, as the Greek god of sleep and dreams, enjoyed, in my opinion, perhaps the least challenging of the divine responsibilities.

conviction that a considerable number of crows had alighted upon the roof, immediately above my room. Were they congregating there in order to enjoy any lingering warmth in the leadwork?

At eight o'clock, Fitz tapped on my door. Greeted me with, "Mornin' Suh—is ya ready fa breakfast?"

My affirmative reply triggered his walking reflex, and I followed him into the musty bowels of the mansion. The meal awaited me in a gloomy anti-chamber to the kitchen, and consisted of a hunk of bread deeply smeared with beef dripping, and a cup of Earl Grey—precisely the sort of food a man needs to prime mind and body for the day ahead!

After eating, I embarked on a short constitutional, which I deemed obligatory prior to the commencement of my cataloguing duties. I set foot outside to admire the morning light and the dew upon the grass.

I am not given to casting aspersions, especially as His Grace had been welcoming, but I found myself dismayed at the condition of the great mansion's exterior. Perhaps the legalities following the late duchess's tragic demise were complicated, such that the migration of capital to which Dr Parsons had alluded, had been stalled in the courts. Heaven forbid that she had departed this world before she had had the opportunity to amend her will in favour of her new husband—or some charlatan had emerged to challenge it. I mention this because the stonework was deeply weathered and the staining more widespread than I had imagined. The windows featured cracked glazing, and the paint that coated the sills, on occasion, did no such thing.

My walk took me to the rear of the house. When I reached the central block that faced the lake, my theorem regarding the flow of capital found itself challenged. A substantial and buttressed wall surrounded an enclosure. The brickwork and mortar—that reached two yards above my head—displaying the hallmarks of recent construction. The location appeared to be directly beneath where I assumed the duke's apartment was located. An iron gate of enviable complication occupied a position at the midpoint of the wall. The oak door behind it denied visual access to the inner sanctum.

"Ah, my good fellow—I see you are admiring my new walled garden."

"Good morning, Your Grace. It looks most impressive, as does the gate, the likes of which I have not previously encountered."

The duke dabbed at his leaking eyes with a silk handkerchief.

"The structure was my dearest Rose's wedding gift to me. The outer gate is the work of the finest craftsmen in her family's employ. It was her fervent wish that this garden be completed post-haste, stocked with scented flowers, and opened to the public. Consequently, I have committed myself single-handedly to that endeavour over the past months—no gardener or other person has been permitted within these walls. Call me sentimental, but I feel in my heart that Her Grace would have appreciated a garden created and nurtured entirely by *my* fair hand. Despite the insubordination of a few recalcitrant botanicals, the grand opening will occur on schedule."

He pointed his walking stick at various metallic representations in the gate. "Morpho butterfly...*maracuja* or you probably know it as the Brazilian passion flower...howler monkey...black caiman...."

"Do I, Your Grace, detect a predilection with South America?"

"In all respects save one, I am equally fascinated by Africa, the Pacific Islands and Amazonia."

"Save one?"

"Magic, young man. It has been my experience that the sorcery of the Amazon basin is perhaps stronger than elsewhere. For example, take the intertwining of these two innocuous plants. Natives call that one *The Vine of the Soul.* The unassuming shrub beside it is known in the Quechua tongue as *chacruna.* When combined, they create a great magic of which I am certain Perkins and his colleagues are ignorant."[30]

My curiosity was aroused, but my enquiry regarding whether he possessed live specimens in the greenhouse, went unanswered. Instead, he described the devil of a time he had had growing alien plants there, of planting them in the garden, and of keeping them alive. He mentioned that he had considered engaging architects to draw up plans for a vast tropical glasshouse. It would have been the twin of the Palm House at Kew Gardens, but apparently this venture had been put on hold for undisclosed reasons.

A horizontal shape, masked by a curtain, occupied the space above the entrance. A cord hung from it.

"I imagine the name of the garden is concealed behind that fabric. May I enquire what moniker you have chosen, Your Grace?"

Now the handkerchief was tasked with capturing the contents of his nostrils.

"After much deliberation, I finally settled upon a name that expresses accurately my sentiments for my dear Rose, and this beautiful garden. A name that I trust will be remembered long after I have joined her in Heaven."

The Golden Rose Garden sprung to mind, but there it remained, as to speak my thoughts seemed impertinent.

As he gazed at the horizon, he was smiling. "This Saturday will mark Her Grace's birthday." After blotting his eyes with the handkerchief, he added, "I will never cease to wonder why The Almighty's Divine Plan required taking her from me in the prime of her life."

"Some feel Cowper put it well, Your Grace."

"You refer to his hymn, *God Moves in a Mysterious Way*?"

"Indeed I do. On occasion, I too find myself perplexed by His plan."

---

[30] The Vine of the Soul... chacruna... The Vine of the Soul... chacruna... that should be lodged in my memory now.

"We are but foolish mortals so let us not dwell on theistic matters. So, I have invited the retired and serving professors, lecturers and senior members of my old faculty to explore the collection on that day. Naturally, their families are invited too, and the children—the more the merrier—will participate in a jolly painted egg hunt in the walled garden, which will ring with laughter and joy. The event will mark the formal opening of both. I hope your busy schedule permits you to join us for a midday commencement, and that you delay your return to Oxford accordingly."

"I would be honoured, Your Grace."

"First Class. As dearest Rose will be observing this joyous event from above, I am certain she will gain comfort knowing that that murderous anaconda failed to prevent both adults and children from enjoying a beautiful garden, the existence of which is entirely due to her generosity."

"*Anaconda*, Your Grace?"

"A gigantic snake, native to the South American continent. The monster seized her when she was composing one of her beautiful poems by the river. It then bound her in its iron coils. When alerted, I ran as best I could, armed with a machete. By the time I had hacked the creature to pieces, it was too late. The beautiful Duchess's ribcage..." he sobbed, "...had been c-c-crushed..."

"What an appalling tragedy, Your Grace. Of course you have my very deepest sympathy. In fact, may I add–"

"An idea occurs to me. Sometimes happenstance intervenes to disrupt the most meticulous plans of wise men and fools alike. It just so happens that I may be called away on business on Friday evening, and be unable to attend. Should this occur, your familiarity with the collection will qualify you to guide my distinguished guests about it, and you could then get the egg hunt underway."

"You may miss the opening?"

"The possibility is a distinct one. And of course, I would be indebted to you if you invited one of the fine ladies present to pull this rope, to reveal the name of the garden.

This should be done at the end of the celebration, when everyone is gathered there. Not before."

"As you wish."

"Another matter: there is an item on my writing desk addressed to your tutor, Riley-Roper."

I wondered if this might be a supper invitation. "May I rely upon you to do me an additional kindness, and ensure he receives it?"

I nodded.[31] "Is there anything else I can do for you, Your Grace? Anything at all…?"

"Make sure the children have a most splendid time at the egg hunt. The eggs will be cunningly concealed, so be sure the young really get stuck in. Announce that one egg contains a gold sovereign, and others, lesser denominations of coinage. Be sure their day ends with plenty of muddy hands and knees. Do you follow?"

"Of course, Your Grace."[32]

He giggled with delight. "Oh, what fun it'll be!"

For the remainder of the day, I was occupied in the Africa Room. I had arrived at Montagu Hall with twenty large sheets of J. Whatman's finest cotton rag paper, rolled inside a tubular map case. Employing a metal ruler, graphite pencil and scissors, I reduced four sheets into a multitude of one inch squares. Employing my late father's Aikin Lambert fountain pen and a copperplate script, I commenced numbering them, starting unsurprisingly, with *1*.

---

[31] Perhaps, if I play my cards well, I might also be invited to attend.
[32] …though forgive me, Your Grace, if I question the veracity of your statement involving concealed coinage.

After determining the most logical manner in which to pair numeral to collectible, I set about gumming or pinning squares to, or beside objects. That task occupied me until late-afternoon, my industry being interrupted for a luncheon of ham hock (a trifle ripe), thickly crusted loaf (a trifle dry) and trifle. Of the promised ale, there was no sign. It was at times like this that I questioned Jumbo Jacobson's philosophy:[33] *cibus pessimus semper est melior quam fame!*[34]

I opened the weighty writing album which had been marked for my attention. Finished in soft black leather, it sported the duke's coat of arms, that comprised a quartered shield containing eagles, roses, coronets, and other such details as now escape me, embossed in gold upon the cover.

I turned to the second page to allow a title to be added to the first by the aforementioned calligrapher, and entered the number *1*. Beside it, I pencilled: *Bronze Pendant of half-moon shape, featuring a skull surrounded by crescents, circles and snakes. Kingdom of Dahomey, mid-Nineteenth Century.*

My work was absorbing, my day long. It occupied me until six minutes after five o'clock, which was when His Grace returned. He studied my work, made a brace of minor amendments, invited me to leave, and locked up.

As it has been my experience that nothing readies the stomach for an excellent evening meal better than an energetic perambulation, I set off towards the lake.

Striding onward, I vowed to continue my cataloguing at a similar pace tomorrow. That would afford me Tuesday to Friday to complete this endeavour, attend—and possibly host—the garden party on Saturday, depart that afternoon,

---

[33] At school, James "Jumbo" Jacobson was famous for consuming any meal placed before him—even if its provenance was undetermined. As the prefects did not permit food to be wasted, he was equally willing to devour other boys' meals.

[34] *Cibus pessimus semper est melior quam fame!* The worst food is always better than hunger!

and return to the museum on Monday morning.[35]

Supper arrived again at seven-thirty, and on this occasion I responded to the knocking by bounding across the room and flinging open the door. My athleticism was rewarded with no more than a glimpse of a young boy dressed in breeches and waistcoat, scurrying down the stairway across the hallway.

"Just a moment!" I shouted but he was off like a rabbit down a hole.

My disappointment at failing to engage him in conversation was as nothing compared with my shock at what was on the menu: mutton stew, stilton and Shrewsbury cake. I imbibed (somewhat optimistically) again, in the hope that the Burgundy had improved its manners since our previous encounter.

The rest of the evening afforded me the opportunity to revisit the events and conversations of the day. Several incongruences troubled me: the first involved the shift in identity of Her Grace's murderer, from a limb-detaching jaguar to a rib-crushing anaconda. Dr Parsons had stated that he recalled vividly the article in the local newspaper, so how could so fundamental and horrific a detail have transmuted over the course of a few months?

Another incongruence involved the late duchess's favourite pastime. Did it involve blending words or colours? Finally, was her killer dispatched with bullet or blade?

My ambition now was to mount a counterattack upon the effects of the fermented Pinot Noir grape, and sustain it

---

[35] Hopefully, having unravelled the mystery of the late duke's death, compelling Dr Parsons to delve deeply into his wallet.

until I had constructed a plausible explanation for the previously mentioned discrepancies.

My best effort took considerable time, and the following shape: I posited that the reporter had invented the details in order to meet a print deadline.[36]

But this explanation did little to assuage my curiosity regarding the possibility that the duke might be unable to attend the opening of a collection that had absorbed him for the greater part of his adult life. Adding his potential absence at a joyous garden party funded by, and no doubt named after, his beloved wife, further deepened the mystery.

There was also the matter of the important item he wished me to deliver to my tutor. Was it a dining invitation—would other academics attend? On reflection, perhaps it was an interesting collectible that related to the slave trade, which did not sit well with the rest of the collection. An illustrated slave cargo manifest, perhaps?[37] A pair of manacles; perchance a fine whip?

Finally, and here I accept I may be guilty of allowing my imagination to run as freely as the steel-pulsed *Manifesto* galloped on 24th March,[38] why would the name of the garden be revealed at the day's conclusion? When vessels are launched, the naming *precedes* the slide down slipway to saline.[39] Would this convention not also apply to a garden?

With no explanation offering itself to these matters, I found myself fretting that the ten shillings remained beyond

---

[36] A second explanation occurred to me: being quite elderly (aged midway between five and six decades), the duke had confused the details on account of his rapidly deteriorating brain.

[37] The illustrated examples attract the highest prices at auction.

[38] I possess an aversion to tossing coin at turf, but having eavesdropped a discussion between four jockeys in the Broken Leg public house, I placed a not insignificant wager upon the aforementioned gelding, in the '99 Aintree Grand National. The superb George Williamson turned my three shillings into fifteen!

[39] As was the case when I attended the launch of HMS Majestic, at Portsmouth, in '95.

reach, while my rental obligations crept ever closer.[40]

I reached for my journal and recorded the more notable events of the day, but that activity failed to divert my thoughts from the sense of urgency regarding my thesis.

As I stared at the gap between the curtains, I recalled Dr Parsons' opinion that *the Alpha Objective involved presenting an original body of work, the Beta should illuminate some aspect of the human condition, and the Gamma necessitated relevance a hundred years hence.* His thesis topic had clearly failed two of three—so how could he expect me to achieve a full house?

I was about to close the journal when I paused to consider the duke's response to my invention, the monopoly-genism. It had evinced that the duke possessed a grand sense of humour, and I might be able to turn that discovery to my advantage. A favourite quotation of Major Dalton sprung to mind:[41] *if you know the enemy and know yourself, you need not fear the results of a hundred battles.* However, I remained mindful that the duke likely knew little more about the local murderer than I, and my efforts could be in vain.

I have always found it challenging to fall asleep around the solstice—the combination of higher mercury and lingering illumination being jointly responsible. Occupying a bed well stuffed with drupes,[42] in a chamber in which the curtains failed to achieve closure, only compounded the problem.

Just as sleep finally did approach, my senses were alerted

---

[40] It was at this moment that, given the complexity and possible danger surrounding identifying the late duke's assassin, I began to wonder whether ten shillings was adequate compensation for my services.

[41] This quotation is attributed to Sun Tzu, a Chinese general, philosopher, and writer (544-496 BC) best remembered for his treatise, *The Art of War*. To this day it is taught at both the Royal Military Academy and the Royal Military College.

[42] Is the coconut a fruit, nut or seed? Perkins (of The Natural History Museum) would no doubt confirm that it is in fact a fibrous one-seeded *drupe*, that performs the function all three.

to an unfamiliar disturbance: a distant pounding. The beat was insistent, it mimicked the pace of my pulse, and over time, accelerated. To my surprise, my heartbeat followed suit.

My attention was then diverted to the return of overhead footsteps. As before, they shared the scratching quality of claw on lead, but on this occasion it struck me that the crows were better coordinating their movements. By which I mean, I could not possibly tell whether four or four-and-twenty black birds had alighted above me. This change of perception arose because what became as apparent as it was unlikely, was that the flock's footsteps now moved in unison.

With this conundrum contributing in no small part to a growing sense of unease, I closed my eyes.[43]

TUESDAY – *note to self: no thesis topic suggested itself to me on Monday. Hopefully the* tabula *will not remain* rasa *for much longer.*[44]

Though the Burgundy had behaved once more with shameless delinquency,[45] by mid-morning I had completed my duties in the Africa Room. Five minutes rest preceded my transporting myself, the writing album, and attendant paraphernalia to the Pacific Islands collection. My endeavours proceeded apace, though occasionally I struggled to describe an item in full. One entry upon which I

---

[43] With Morpheus eventually addressing the first, but not second, of his divine responsibilities.

[44] With apologies to Virgil, Catullus, Propertius, *et al* for playing fast and loose with their language. *Tabula rasa.* A clean slate.

[45] Compelling me to add Dionysus, the Greek god of wine, to a growing list of underperforming deities at Montagu Hall.

temporized read: *Wooden Fijian Totokia War Club—[probably] inlaid with bone—the former property of a Chief or Priest.*

The remainder of the day flowed with few interruptions, though luncheon was, for reasons that requite no elaboration, a grand disappointment. I finished work late again: at twelve minutes after five, which was when His Grace entered.

"Apologies for my tardiness but I was occupied nurturing a simply marvellous Australian plant in my greenhouse that I will transfer to the walled garden tomorrow. Being more comfortable in that country's rainforests than in a Northamptonshire flowerbed, I fear my efforts with *Dendrocnide moroides* might come to naught.[46] We shall see."

He studied my entries.

"Your work is excellent but it does contain errors in respect of item 282—the Totokia War Club—the inlays are not bone, they are human teeth. Also, please record that it is made from a hardwood occurring in those parts called *vesi*. The item was the property of a prominent chief who was persuaded to part with it in exchange for my excellent Adolphus Busch pocket knife. This should have been a worthwhile transaction as such clubs are believed to contain the life force or *mana* of their victims. The more victims, the more mana—and the chief swore on the Bible that he had dispatched twenty-seven Tongans with it."

After a pause, he sighed. "Regrettably, my rigorous experiments proved that the shameless scoundrel sold me a counterfeit."

"If I might be so bold as to make a suggestion, Your Grace?"

He studied me before answering. "Which is…?"

---

[46] Why must gardeners insist on complicating life with their employment of binomial nomenclature when most plants—no doubt this one as well—have perfectly usable English names?

"Perhaps you should have ordered the club from Harrods."

"Are you being serious, young man?"

"Well, their advertisements claim they can obtain anything in the world, and you will be fully reimbursed should you not be delighted with your purchase."

He smiled. "Most amusing! From Harrods?" He threw his head back and laughed. "To think I've wasted years travelling to the most inhospitable corners of the globe when a couple of trips to Knightsbridge would have sufficed. Ha, ha, ha!"

I laughed with him.

"Parsons told me you were an entertaining fellow. I'm glad I engaged you—I've been meaning to enquire: room comfortable? Food to your liking?"

"Both first class."

"Excellent! Now, returning to that Fijian scoundrel...it would be unjust to leave you with the impression that he was entirely devoid of positive qualities. For example, he employed a most thought-provoking stratagem for punishing his enemies. Can you guess how he achieved his ends?"

"Via the administration of a blue-ringed octopus bite?"

"Such a death is far too rapid. I will provide a clue: his preferred technique drew out the suffering indefinitely."

"He employed black magic, via a fiendish curse, perhaps?"

"Excellent suggestion, but incorrect again, I'm afraid."

Before I could volunteer a third suggestion, he said, "Though he had not profited from a proper education, he was in fact an advocate of the scientific method. Sea snakes, stonefish, lionfish, cone shells...we conducted experiments with them all, in search of the most efficacious venom, while sharing anecdotes that made us laugh heartily throughout."

"He sounds like memorable entertainment, Your Grace—does this not qualify him to dine at the same table as your good self and Dr Riley-Roper?"

"Excellent idea!" After a moment, he added, "I've been

thinking what a talented fellow you are, Robert."

"Thank you Your Grace. And may I add that when I woke in my warm and comfortable bed this morning, after another sublimely restful night, I was reflecting upon how much I was enjoying this assignment."

He smiled. "I have told the staff to ensure you are taken care of. You can't expect a fellow to do a good day's work after a bad night's sleep."

Some twenty minutes later, I was enjoying a balmy evening as I strode across the parkland, approaching the woods. Mindful of Dr Parsons' warning, I was content to skirt its boundary.

My attention wandered when I heard barking, and peering ahead, I recognised the young woman who had been seated at the fountain. Though some considerable distance separated us, I could make out her lightness of step, slim figure, and the long dress that flowed about her. The straw hat had again been employed to guard against sunburn. The dog, spirits high, bound alongside its mistress, leaping for the throwing-stick she carried.

The woman's progress proved deceptively rapid for no injection of pace on my part diminished the separation between us. Her route altered suddenly as she closed on the lake, and mine followed suit. As she approached a gap in the reeds, the waterfowl—swan, mallard, coot, moorhen—paddled towards her with determination. It was evident that the parties were well acquainted; from the birds' behaviour, I inferred that they anticipated the imminent arrival of tossed bread crusts.

My musings were violently interrupted when I inhaled an

extraordinarily pungent odour that instigated paroxysms of such intensity that I wretched. They say that we never forget a memorable olfaction; hence, I was immediately transported to the occasion on which I encountered a decomposing ewe upon Bodmin Moor.

By holding my breath and advancing with extreme caution, I was successful in identifying the origin of this contemporaneous effluvium. It was disquieting to be faced with a dead stag whose ribs and plumbing were exposed.

Closer inspection of the gaping cavity precluded any explanation involving a shotgun—or indeed an elephant gun. I hurried away pondering what exceptional misfortune could have befallen so strong an animal and, assuming it was murdered, whether it was by the same hand that had butchered the sheep. Perhaps it *had* died a natural death, and foxes had been tearing at it. In any case, what was difficult to reconcile was the errant performance of the gamekeeper, who should have removed the carcass days ago.

I had allowed this gruesome event to absorb me for a minute or two. When I again focused upon the perimeter of the lake, hopeful of seeing the elegant lady again, of her, and her canine companion, there was no sign.

The young fellow who arrived outside my door failed to observe me, on account of the hallway curtain I sheltered behind. I had chosen my position with care, and as he placed the tray outside my door, it took but a few steps to position myself at the top of the staircase—preventing his escape.

"Good evening. A minute of your time, if I may?"

The look of surprise on his sallow face was a sight to behold.

"I'm sorry, Suh. Mutt'n, stilt'n 'n that stale cake's all we 'ave royt nar."

I could tell he had brains. "And your name is…?"

"Tommy, Suh."

"Well Tommy, my line of enquiry involves another matter. Is there a problem with the crows here? Why must they congregate on the roof and wake me?"

His eyes bulged with alarm. Voice trembling, he said, "Oi dunno nothin' 'bout na crows, Suh."

"The treble negative aside, why doesn't the gamekeeper poison them? And I encountered a rotting deer today. The man should be dismissed without delay!"

"'Is Grace don't neva employ no keepa, Suh."[47]

Mindful of my approaching rent, I determined that this particular pump required priming. I handed him threepence.

"Anything strange afoot, Tommy?"

"Suh?"

"Crows, carcasses, a persistent thumping noise in the night…I believe you know what I'm talking about."

"Well Suh, you're not only un who don't sleep proppa, on account o' t'…drummin'.'"

"From whence does it originate?"

"From 'is Grace's 'partment, Suh. That's woy 'e makes Mrs Biggins put powda in ya woyne. Ta 'elp ya sleep. 'Scuse me, Suh. Ize best be off 'fore ize missed."

"Good lord! A *sleeping draft* in my wine?"

He correctly judged the extent to which this news distracted me, and sprang forward. Jinxing to his left, I moved to block him, but a neat duck accompanied by a sidestep took him beneath my flailing arm. He shot down the stairs like a rabbit down a hole—this time with a business of ferrets in close pursuit.[48]

"And lad, there's another threepence for you should you

---

[47] It has to be said: what Tommy's grammar lacked in definitude, it compensated for with consistency.

[48] The collective noun pertaining to a group of ferrets is indeed a *business*. The next time this knowledge wins you a pint of ale in your local hostelry, I trust you will drink my health.

choose to share what you know about the nocturnal footsteps," I shouted after him.

"Astonishing," I muttered, comparing a level of athleticism last observed in Herbert Borthwick—known as the *Merton Meteor*—who'd held (without challenge) the university position of rugby fly-half three years running.[49]

When I had re-entered my room, I lifted the glass to the gaslight, and spied an accumulation of crystals at the junction of bowl and stem.

Opening the window, the liquid was disembogued into the guttering. I left it open in a forlorn gesture to encourage a stirring of the air.

Later still, I lay in bed. I pondered the duke's motivation to manipulate my sleep and for exercising with that percussion instrument late at night. I entered these concerns in my journal. My knowledge was disgracefully incomplete on the subject of native drumming, but I attempted to retrieve the few introductory facts I retained on the subject:

If I recalled correctly, drumming was practised by a native quasi-religious figure known as a *shaman*. The word, if memory served me, arrived in Europe in 1692 with the publication of the Netherlander Nicolaes Witsen's *Noord en Oost Tataryen*, which detailed his encounters with the Samoyedic and Tungusic speakers of Siberia.

The word is likely a derivation of the Tungusic *šaman*, or later Sym Evenki *šamán*, and means *one who knows*. As the book was written in Witsen's native Dutch (and his use of the semi-colon and apostrophe were somewhat inconsistent),[50] I acknowledge that there were passages with which I struggled. I learned however, that via drumming, the shaman would experience what was described as *an altered state of consciousness*, during which he entered what he referred

---

[49] *Merton*, as in the Oxford college he attended, rather than the London borough, Norfolk village, or Australian railway station, he did not.

[50] I derive little pleasure in adding that on occasion, also incorrect.

to as *the spirit world.*

In 1697 or 1698, a merchant from Lübeck named Adam Brand published *Driejaarige Reize naar China,* an account that addressed similar matters. I read it in its original tongue (though a translation was available). It remains my conclusion that drumming was practised by shamans throughout the world for magico-religious purposes and that present chroniclers fall well short of understanding its purpose.[51]

Concerning the birds above me: keeper or no keeper, surely His Grace could instruct someone to scatter arsenic-laced bread across the length and breadth of the roof, which is how some deal with this problem.[52]

My window was still open, but the night was uncommonly still, preventing the circulation of fresh air about my chamber. I was comparing the absolute silence of Montagu Hall with my noisy rooms at Oxford when my ears beheld an unfamiliar sound. By concentrating, I confirmed it was not the work of my imagination and soon enough its increase in volume confirmed the same. In fact, there was no mistaking it: the crunch of wheels on gravel.

I substituted a horizontal for vertical inclination, and made towards the door with haste. Unfortunately, my toe collided with the iron of the bed leg, which brought tears to my eyes and words to my lips that I scarcely knew formed a portion of my lexicon. I left my room behind, traversed the corridor, and came to rest at a window whose alignment was suitable for my purpose.

---

[51] As a matter of priority, immediately upon my return to Oxford, I pledged to better acquaint myself with this fascinating subject.

[52] A further advantage of this method is that should a fox then devour the crow's carcase, the poison is transferred. (Had I been able to make a humorous reference to killing two birds with one stone, I would surely have done so. In compensation, allow me to offer the following: *where do foxes shop when their tails falls off? Answer: at the re-tail store!*)

I arrived with seconds to spare. The moon glinted upon the hansom that had pulled up on the driveway below. It ran no lights. A moment later a door creaked open below me, and the figure of a large man emerged from the building. A cape draped about him, he proceeded to limp towards the cab in a most secretive manner. The driver handed over what compared dimensionally with the wooden box that houses a magnum of wine. What may have been money changed hands. Glancing about him, the hunched figure returned indoors as the cab made its departure.

I was about to make mine when the scruffy dog emerged from the shadows and traversed the gravel to the location previously occupied by the hansom. It sniffed the ground, whined, then looked about. As I turned to leave, the unfortunate mutt threw its head back and howled.

On re-entering my room, I considered what I had witnessed. Why was the cab running no lights, and why had the duke appeared anxious of remaining unseen? As for the item itself—in the unlikely event that it was a bottle of fine wine, it certainly wasn't intended for my consumption. If it was not wine, what exactly was it?

These and other thoughts were recorded in the journal before I allowed my imagination to get better of me: I felt that the animal had been waiting for the carriage, as if it had anticipated the arrival of someone it loved. Have we not all heard of the sleeping dog that wakes from its slumber to settle by the front door, three minutes before its master returns from work? Though mistaken in its conviction, I recorded the event lest time prove it of significance, closed the journal and placed it upon the bedside table.

WEDNESDAY – *note to self: only three full days remain, and I have made limited progress. I must refocus my efforts to avoid failure, the consequences of which would be dire.*

I consider myself fastidious, which is why I added what some would consider superfluous detail to the final sentence of the Tuesday stanza. I refer specifically to mention of the closing of the journal. This matter warrants scrutiny because on waking, I was instantly aware of a curious odour; not strong, not unpleasant…simply *curious*. The air had about it the smell of damp paperboard.

I feared I had overturned my water glass in the night, and its contents had flooded the journal. This concern was dispelled promptly when I remembered that the ancillaries provided for my comfort at Montagu Hall did not extend to a jug of water and receptacle. Inspection of the journal confirmed its dryness. However, it lay open and appeared to have been rotated through a half circle. Had I allowed my imagination free rein, I might have created an explanation that involved someone browsing its pages while I slept. But my bedroom door was locked and with my key still *in situ*, the employment of a second key from outside was impossible. What also remained unexplained—regrettably my imagination made no contribution in this regard—was the origin of the odour.

My mood—like the weather—was decidedly overcast. Both showed some improvement after breakfast.

At nine o'clock, I was passing through the Amazonia collection, on my way to commencing my duties in the Pacific Islands Room, which I estimated would occupy me until the afternoon. An open window beside the stuffed condor encouraged the ingress of air, which further elevated my spirits. With effort, I had pushed the mysteries of the previous night to the back of my mind, justifying the duke's odd conduct as aristocratic eccentricity. After all, was it not a source of considerable amusement that the Earl of ————— enjoyed nothing better than to observe his stablehands engaging in bouts of naked wrestling? And what of the orchestra Viscount ——————— commanded play the score of that Tchaikovsky ballet to his swans, to encourage them to lay?

However, my musings were interrupted by a most unexpected sight. The brass-framed display container located in the centre of the room had not altered its location. Nor had it altered its design. What had altered was its status, which had transitioned from empty to occupied. And the occupant possessed a most singular appearance.

Behind the glass I observed what in terms of topography, appeared to share the general configuration of a toffee apple. For those unfamiliar with this tooth-rotting temptation, imagine, if you will, a spherical object.

Approximately twelve inches of stick emerged from its base. However, I was unable to ascertain the nature of the upper portion because it was shrouded in a hood of what resembled chamois leather. This was held in place with a plaited rope resembling horsehair, which my mother may have confirmed originated from the Argentine *Criollo* breed, on account of its pale colour.

The item was apparently precious because the locking mechanism of the glass door—comprising bolts top and bottom—had been secured with padlocks. A black wax seal, that incorporated the duke's heraldic components, completed the security measures.

"An excellent morning to you, Robert! I see that you have happened upon our new arrival."

"Good morning, Your Grace. I was wondering what this fascinating collectible might be."

"Fascinating it indeed is. Took the devil of a time to arrive, though. At one point I feared it had been mislaid in transit. However, as I frequently remind myself, you cannot hurry these things. As for your enquiry: concealed beneath that hood is the skull of a giant Amazonian river otter transformed into a magical fetish by a senior craftsman of the Aguaruna people. The hair that maintains that leather hood in place originates from that most indolent creature, the sloth. The strands have been washed, bleached by the sun, and spun into a fine yarn in order that it may be plaited so."

"I counted thirteen plaits. Is that number significant?"

"If I had knowledge of such matters, I would surely share it with you."

"If you might indulge my curiosity further, why *is* the otter skull shrouded by that hood, Your Grace?"

"Bright light will degrade the plant dyes with which it is decorated. It takes time until they, and the herbs within the cranium, are fully cured. Which is why the container is entirely airtight."

"I understand."

The duke smiled, "If you'll excuse me..." He walked over to the window and closed it.

"I appreciate you taking the trouble to describe the item to me, Your Grace. Would you wish me to catalogue it accordingly?"

"As I said before, I will enter it myself."

I completed my work in the Pacific Islands Room shortly after four-thirty, which left me thirty minutes until the duke's arrival, and two full days to devote to the Amazonia collection. I reclined in my chair and closed my eyes, and the usual concerns flooded my brain.

For the first time, I entertained the possibility that I may fail to unravel a knot that made its Gordian counterpart appear, by comparison, straightforward. To prevent this concern overwhelming me, I embarked upon a tangential exercise: I asked myself whether, by some other means, I might extract benefit from the assignment.

To leave without a thesis topic and forfeit the ten shilling would be doubly ruinous, but did some scholastic opportunity exist that I had to this moment overlooked? The first step of the Scientific Method involves asking a question. But what might that question be? I revisited my notes, alighting upon a passage. I brought my palms together with a resounding clap. This vulgar gesture was joined by another—a coarse bellow: "Of course—yes, that would work handsomely!" Even in my moment of triumph, the uncouth nature of my celebration was not lost upon me.

It was, however, a final thought that added to my sense of satisfaction: just imagine *their* surprise!

Reinvigorated, I decided to stretch my limbs. My amble transported me through the Africa collection and back to the Amazonia Room, where I dallied before the hooded fetish, luxuriating in my new stratagem. My idea would require some adjustments, but with application—

My thoughts ended most abruptly. Despite the locked and sealed nature of the container, one of the plaits had unravelled.

My supper arrived via tray in the gnarled graspers of Fitz. His lack of conversation made Tommy, by comparison, appear garrulous. I did hazard a casual enquiry about the safety of a ramble in the woods, but discovered that his temper was as frayed as his cuffs. Consequently, the fleeting idea of investing a further threepence in my portfolio of Montagu Hall mysteries was abandoned, along with any hopes of procuring information from this surly fellow.

After I'd poured away the wine and consumed what I could of the food, I left the tray outside and retired early to devote my time to my thoughts. A brace of summers ago I had enjoyed a pleasant walk along the banks of Devonshire's River Torridge, greenheart fly rod in hand.[53] A portion of that afternoon had been occupied observing nature at its most raw, as an otter struggled to subdue an eel it had dragged onto the bank. While one writhed and the other rolled, I had opportunity to observe the shape of the mammal's head. Recalling it now, I would describe it as elongated, flattened, and tapered—a description I presumed would serve appositely for the bones within. So, for what reason would the skull of that creature's Amazonian cousin, when deprived of muscle, sinew and fur, adopt an alternative configuration?

My musings continued as I considered the relevance of Darwin's thesis in this instance. Perhaps, following random mutations, the head of the giant otter of Amazonia had evolved a spherical aspect, which better served it when hunting the denizens of that expansive watercourse.

However, when I recalled a family of stuffed Californian sea otters I had observed in the Pitt Rivers—which resembled the Torridge specimen in all aspects save volume—I realised that in whichever locked chest the resolution to this latest mystery lay, it certainly wasn't the one labelled *evolutionary biology.*

I reconsidered the size of the skull and deduced that the duke had meant to say a *young* otter, as the object shared its dimensions with, I suppose, the head of a domestic cat.

But there was another matter demanding consideration: I was unaware that the Aguaruna people dyed bone, or incorporated plaited sloth hair in their fetishes. This mystery certainly provided content for a forthcoming conversation with Dr Parsons. Though no doubt interesting, I recognised that such a dialogue would be unlikely to edge me closer to

---

[53] I will go on record that in my opinion, greenheart remains an entirely superior rod construction material to the split cane creations brandished by our *nouveau riche* angling companions.

the contents of his wallet.

These concerns contributed to a fitful sleep that was again interrupted at the appointed hour. The drumming woke me, but of the crows, there was no sign. As I lay in that gloomy chamber, the moonlight permitted me to distinguish shapes: the bed upright responsible for my blackened toe, the chair, and the dressing table were all visible in the gloom. In an attempt to shield myself from the moonlight and gain a degree of comfort from the mattress, I turned on my side with my back facing the window.

What transpired before I closed my eyes resembled the extinguishing of a gaslight, for suddenly the room was plunged into darkness. That event alone would have severely jarred my nerves, but it was joined by a muffled commotion that originated from the vicinity of the window ledge.

I lay frozen, my pulse accelerating until it outpaced the drum beats. Someone or something large enough to block the moonlight stood at the window. Cold droplets of perspiration sprung from my brow. Holding my breath served only to make my pounding heart more audible. No power on earth could have equipped me with the courage to turn and inspect who, or what, stood but ten feet away.

Just when I imagined my terror could rise no further, it doubled. Then doubled again. I heard a thud, and footsteps—that approached my bed. My first thought was to pull the covers over my head. But I rejected this ploy lest the movement alerted my visitor to my presence. If I remained perfectly still, I reasoned—no I *prayed*—my unwelcome guest might conclude that the room was unoccupied, turn, and depart.

My prayer went unanswered. Though I was now conscious of someone or something standing over me, I felt wholly uncommitted to opening my eyes or rolling over to confront my visitor with my ventral aspect.

Indeed, such was the extent of my panic that I cannot estimate with confidence for how long this *impasse* persisted, but eventually I could hold my breath no longer. I breathed deeply. What I was more certain of, was the origin of the odour that that action dragged into my nostrils.

My stomach clenched and I feared I'd wretch. As I battled to prevent a convulsion, the footsteps resumed and transported my unwelcome visitor back towards the window. The moonlight was restored with the same suddenness with which it had been extinguished. The drumming reached a crescendo. Then, without warning, silence returned.

Muscle by muscle my body relaxed. Finally, I could think. As my bedroom was situated on the upper floor, I concluded that my visitor had either employed a rope to lower him- or itself, had bounded thirty feet vertically, or had gained access to my room via a ladder.

There was also the matter of the odour. I had smelt it before, and recently: it was the stench of putrid venison.

I lit a candle before reaching for the Bible that Dr Parsons had given me. I flipped the pages with gusto until my eyes alighted on a chapter in The Book of Isaiah that seemed to convey a message about protection. I read it aloud, conscious of the tremble in my voice:

> *"So do not fear, for I am with you; do not be dismayed, for I am your God. I will strengthen you and help you; I will uphold you with my righteous right hand. All who rage against you will surely be ashamed and disgraced; those who oppose you will be as nothing and perish. "*

When finally dawn's fingers probed the room, I dared close my eyes. With Herculean effort, I forced my mind to cease its efforts to explain the night's visitation. Eventually an agitated form of sleep engulfed me.

THURSDAY – *note to self: the tipping point where concern gives way to fear has been reached, as the hourglass empties…*

It was not unexpected that my cognitive processes bore meagre resemblance to the morning's meteorology, which was clear and bright.

Seated at my cataloguing station, I concluded that two positive elements had birthed from last night's experience. The former was the cognizance that the ten shillings was back on the table; the latter involved a palpable awareness of the comfort I had been afforded by reading The Good Book. I elected to delve deeper into its pages tonight…in the hope that it might help me reconcile a personal dilemma that had occupied my thoughts for the past two years.

The squeak of an unoiled wheel and most jovial voice interrupted my thoughts, so I approached the window to ascertain their origin. His Grace walked ahead of a scruffy individual, who pushed a well-stacked wheelbarrow. I presumed the second man was a member of the gardening staff.

Were I a parliamentarian, I would immediately have introduced a Private Member's Bill legislating that any Savile Row tailor supplying cloth such as the duke now sported, be compelled to also supply white walking canes for those blinded by its violent assault upon the colour spectrum.[54]

The pair drew level with my vantage point. His Grace afforded me a cordial wave, which was accompanied by an enthusiastic: *a very good morning to you, Robert!*

The gardener appeared vastly uncommitted to his

---

[54] In which habitat would *that* assemblage of colours disguise the wearer? Had the duke commissioned this kaleidoscopic cacophony for those occasions on which he partook of the botanical delirium, *Tabernanthe iboga*? The tweed would probably blend with the other-worldly colours encountered on that hallucinogenic journey, and serve to keep him unnoticed by the fiends and demons that have previously been referenced as inhabiting those terrifying realms.

employer's merriment, which struck me as unsporting, on account that the barrow was bursting with brightly painted eggs. Some were tiny, such as might be laid by the flighty wren; others rivalled the dimensions of the mighty ostrich's reproductive contribution.

Master and serf continued on their journey, halting outside the walled garden's entrance. The duke unlocked the gate and entered, leaving the gardener standing outside. I returned to my work.

Thirty minutes later, I was overwhelmed by a most peculiar sensation. I felt certain that I was being observed by person or persons unknown. This feeling was accompanied by a degree of apprehension. Walking around the room, I confirmed all was as it should be. Then I closed my eyes, allowing my head to turn this way and that, much as a weather vane responds to a breeze, in an attempt to ascertain from which direction this sense of scrutiny originated. When I opened them, I found myself facing the stuffed condor.

Under normal circumstances, I would have chastised myself for allowing my imagination to get the better of me. But last night's shenanigans had left their mark, and they do say that to forgive is divine. Hence, I forgave myself my indulgence, walked over to the bird, and confirmed that its eyes remained bound by linen. Then I adjusted its alignment so that it faced the wall.

This action had the desired effect and allowed me to work uninterrupted until Tommy arrived with a tray. The apologetic look on his face hardly lessened my disappointment regarding the tray's cargo.

"How are you, Tommy?" I managed with great cheeriness, hoping to engage him in a conversation that would achieve twin objectives: to elicit information and not cost me threepence.

Instead of answering, he stared, mouth agape, at the stuffed bird, no doubt contemplating its new orientation. So engrossed was he in this activity, that the repetition of my enquiry proved no more successful than the original. He then departed in a considerable hurry.

All of which would have given me pause for thought, had it not been for a final event that had literally been unravelling before my eyes. In an effort to treat my optics to an alternative panorama to the catalogue album, I found myself focusing upon the duke's most recent acquisition. It was much as I remembered it—the exception being a significant one: more of the plaits had unravelled.

As I confirmed that no less than four of the original thirteen had now unwound, I found myself questioning the craftsmanship of the Aguaruna tribesman who was responsible for its manufacture. Surely some glue or paste, thread or lacquer could have been employed to better secure the braids.

This idea occasioned a closer inspection which revealed a robust thread of similar colour to the plaits—hence my failure to observe it previously—had indeed been bound around the termination of the interweaves. The mysteries that engulfed me centred on identifying the process by which that thread had burst, leaving portions of it lying on the container's base, and how, in an airtight chamber, an energy existed that could be responsible for the unwinding. As I grappled with these riddles, I noticed I had commenced perspiring.

My supper was delivered by Fitz once again, which meant the threepence remained in my pocket. Whatever lay ahead, I felt it should not be faced on an empty stomach, so the stew, cheese and cake were forced down. I was tempted to drink the wine, and had even considered enquiring if a second might be procured. This scheme might guarantee a night of uninterrupted sleep, but would almost certainly deprive me of the opportunity to garner new information. Consequently, the contents of the glass met a familiar fate.

Settled in a chair and breathing deeply in an effort to relax, I soon found myself at a fork in the road I thought I had left behind two years previously. Then I spoke, as if giving voice to my perturbation would better carry my words to the ears of The Almighty.

"Lord, why did you allow my parents to perish in the house fire? My mother was the most loving woman. My father devoted his life to serving you and doubled his congregation in a year. By *moving in a mysterious way*—forgive me, but it has to be said—you undermined my faith."

I recited The Lord's Prayer, as if such an action might fill the room with religious energy, which in turn might protect me. On completion of this exercise, I looked at the ceiling and said, "You see, Lord, I am *trying*."

When I was ready for bed, I kneeled beside it. Three passages I had previously identified in The Good Book were delivered in my most compelling voice.[55]

I added an invocation of my own invention that I confess wandered somewhat. It opened strongly enough, imploring the Lord to protect me from evil now and always. In return, I undertook to be a stranger no longer at The University Church of St Mary the Virgin, and committed to reserve the first and third Sunday of each month for that purpose.

I finished with a request that I succeed in uncovering whatever was afoot at Montagu Hall—and that the ten shillings would be mine in time to pay my rent.

After some reflection, I added a postscript, if such a thing may be added to a prayer: I requested that should I survive whatever perils lay ahead, I would reconsider

---

[55] I would go so far as to venture that my words were well articulated, the tone rose and fell at appropriate junctures, and the performance was wrapped in a fitting blanket of solemnity. Without doubt, my delivery compared favourably with the monotonous sermons delivered by the vicars I had encountered over the years. Had I, in fact, missed my calling in life?

devoting the remainder of my life to serving God, by entering the Church.

After some *further* reflection, I wondered if I was being a trifle insubordinate when I contrived an additional postscript that invited The Almighty to plant the idea in Dr Parsons' mind that perhaps my efforts justified a more generous imbursement of not ten, but fifteen shillings. *Nihil ausum, nihil impetratum!*[56]

My swirling thoughts prevented sleep—and turning the mattress over confirmed only that the former topside was no less lumpy than the former underside.

Unable to sleep, I amended my journal by gaslight, and watched the rising moon. It helped little that the heavenly body ascending the night sky reminded me of the climbing blade of the guillotine...

My reflections pivoted to fond memories: I recalled the comfort of living in a vicarage, and the respect my family enjoyed in that thatched Wiltshire village. Nor would I forget the majestic Priory Church of St. Mary, St. Katharine and All Saints, that was consecrated in 1361.

Following an uplifting Evensong or Communion, the faithful would gather outside the church—like Trafalgar Square pigeons on a discarded pickle sandwich—to jostle for my father's attention. It was undeniable: the life of a vicar would be a most pleasant one!

I found myself trifling with the subject of my first sermon, and had given form to its lofty premise, but my contemplations were immediately redirected when the drumming commenced...

---

[56] *Nihil ausum, nihil impetratum!* Nothing ventured, nothing gained!

Major Dalton's classes were unlike others, on account of his predilection for what many would describe as *preaching*—an activity that occupied the final ten minutes of every lesson.

He was well-travelled, well-read, and supremely valorous, having been decorated with the Victoria Cross, which no doubt fuelled his world view, which remained as inflexible as his back.

The homily inevitably comprised four parts: the opening, which involved "My shining stars, there comes a time in every man's life..."; the middle, which presented a day of reckoning or a significant obstacle to overcome. For the major, this occurred during the Second Anglo-Afghan War.[57] Third came the critical choice—whether to اڼ تخاب يو: ووڼ بڼ تى: اخ ت يار دوهم or وک رئ م بارزه او ودرب رئ.[58] Finally, Major Dalton would explore the consequences of both courses of action. Brandish-Russell and the Smellings twins were given to hum *God Save the Queen* throughout these monologues. The damage to the major's eardrums, caused by the repeated retort of cannon, musket, and his wife's relentless admonitions, rendered him entirely oblivious to their harmonies.

Mindful of Major Dalton's teachings, I repositioned the chair to face the window, which as a precaution, remained unopened. A secondary precaution was employed: the bedroom door was agape lest my bravery deserted me. My throat was dry and my heart pounded as I awaited my nocturnal visitor. With both hands I gripped the Bible.

Soon enough my patience was rewarded. Firstly, I was aware of a dark shape that slid across the face of the moon. A subsequent pass brought it closer—rendering it

---

[57] When leading a heroic charge of the 92nd Highlanders, a Pashtun tribesman armed with a *jezail* flintlock, put a lead ball through his eye.

[58] I have reproduced these quotations in their original Pashto, as Major Dalton was wont to do, on account of his unwavering commitment to that region and its traditions. The former translates as: *Option One: stand and fight*. The latter translates as: *Option Two: flee.*

considerably larger. A third was joined by a flapping commotion as an enormous bird—black as the night itself—alighted on the window ledge. Talons grappled with timber until purchase was gained. The vast wings were folded. Separated only by a thin pane of glass, its head was but feet from mine. My instinct was to scream, drop the book, and exercise وٹ بِد تِی :اخ دَ یار دوھ with all possible haste. *Qui pugnat et fugit, alio die pugnat!*[59]

However, the terror that had seized me rendered me completely immobile. Through half-closed eyes, I beheld the grotesque creature. The head was repulsive—bald and dull, topped with a sizeable flap of flesh. The feathered collar that circled its neck glowed pale in the moonlight; the same source of illumination cast the creature's shadow across the length of the room.

Of course I immediately recognised it as the twin of the stuffed bird in the Amazonia collection, but for what purpose was an inhabitant of the peaks of South America alighting upon the windowsill of a grand mansion in Northamptonshire, England, in 1899?

The bird continued to watch me. When it tilted its head, I experienced the curious notion that it was thinking. And I was thinking too: I knew little about condors, except that they were related to the African vulture, which dined primarily on carrion. Did this monstrous avian share its cousin's dietary proclivities? If so, perhaps I was not facing imminent and mortal danger.

At that moment it tapped the glass with its beak and tilted its head once again. Was it attempting to communicate? Did it wish to be…invited inside?

Throughout this episode, my fear had made me senseless to the drumming. As my stomach unknotted, that awareness returned and I recognised that the sound was approaching its crescendo. My list of compelling reasons for not inviting the

---

[59] *Qui pugnat et fugit, alio die pugnat!* He who fights and runs away, lives to flee another day!

bird to join me had reached eleven when the next event rendered that list redundant.

The bird turned to face the source of the disturbance, then pitched itself into the void. The wings—tipped with long, feathered fingers—beat the night air in a great commotion, and it disappeared from sight. I leapt up and opened the window, leaning out as far as I dared, to see its dark silhouette gliding adjacent to the building's facade. Light warmed the rear of the columns in front of the duke's apartment. It was outside a lit window that the bird alighted. The drumming ceased. The window opened. It entered.

I waited and watched. Finally, the fowl reappeared. It launched itself into the night, in the direction of the woods. I went to bed soon thereafter, with, naturally, much on my mind. Indeed my journal entry—competed with a shaking hand—stretched to seven pages. It included questions such as why had the creature called on me, before visiting the duke? Had it been trained to respond to the drumming? What business did it have about the estate? And of course, was it responsible for the dead stag?

In waking, I recognised that sleep had eventually engulfed me. In fact, it took some considerable time to drag myself free from a disturbing dream that returned throughout the day.[60] Before I share the details, permit me to state that I understand that many dreams are considered to be little more than the mind processing events of the recent past.

---

[60] Did Morpheus's remit allow for nightmares? Perhaps Greek gods experience a reduced sense of obligation towards those who do not converse in their language?

In the dream, I had indeed opened the window and the bird had entered. The discussions I had had regarding the slave trade might explain why, in my dream, the bird was tethered via chain to a weighty iron ball. Additional details include that the bird leapt and struggled, but no amount of effort would allow it to gain flight. Blood oozed from where the iron shackle ground on bone, and in the dream, the same scarlet tinged the dawn sky. The lake and woodland of the estate had been replaced with the jagged, snow-capped peaks of the Andes. Other members of the condor's kin soared amongst the clouds on outstretched wings, and the chained bird, head raised, called to them in a series of pitiful squeaks. One swooped low, as if to inspect the prisoner, which became quite frantic in its efforts to escape.

The dream ended soon after the bird tilted its head at me. Curiously, I was able to understand what it desired, though it communicated in silence. It asked me—no it *begged* me—for its freedom.

FRIDAY – *note to self: the plan I have formulated is not without fault, but I must make my move today, or it will be too late.*

I rushed breakfast. Important, in fact *critical* as the ten shillings remained,[61] I now experienced an all-consuming curiosity to solve a riddle that rivalled the Hampton Court Maze in complexity—and I had until lunchtime tomorrow to do so. Entering the Amazonia Room, I felt a pronounced sense of unease, and immediately turned the stuffed bird to

---

[61] Or whatever the amount with which I, with The Good Lord's intervention, persuaded Dr Parsons to part.

face away from me—though I recognised the gross illogic unbefitting an Oxford-educated man—of associating this stuffed creature with its nocturnal, extant duplicate.

On inspecting the hooded fetish, I caught my breath because more plaits had unwoven. I waited until I had calmed myself sufficiently to commence my work. Then, with trembling hands, I set about cataloguing.

The morning passed with punishing hebetude.[62] At noon, I heard cheerful humming and the arrival of the wheelbarrow. His Grace and the gardener passed the window and again, the squeaking vehicle was fully laden with gaily painted eggs. On this occasion, however, I noticed another accoutrement of the gardening trade: a pairs of arm-length gloves, of thick leather construction, lay draped across the contents.

"Good day, Robert!" the duke shouted.

I was about to respond when I noticed the young woman again. She stood thirty feet behind the duke—both he and the gardener appeared unaware of her presence. As I studied her, she turned slowly toward me. From that distance, the straw hat veiled her features but it did not veil the intensity of a feeling that flooded through me. I have never previously considered whether a smile can be *felt*, if it is not *seen*, but in that moment a dizziness permeated my body and the mission at Montagu Hall was all but forgotten...

"I said, good day Robert!"

With much effort and little conviction, I returned the duke's salutation, as I marvelled at the power of her stare. The feeling, however, slipped from my grasp like a favourite dream. His next verbalisation dragged me back to the present.

---

[62] A favourite word of Major Dalton, used frequently in the context of a modestly athletic assemblage of youth that comprised the school's 3rd Fifteen rugby team, (of which I was the proud full-back) that he coached to a long and distinguished string of defeats.

"Been meaning to ask you: have you solved the mystery of the Fijian chief's preferred method of punishing his enemies?"

As I watched the woman depart, I feared I might not see her again. This concern trumped any wish on my part for commencing a game of *Twenty Questions* with the duke.

"I apologise but other matters have been occupying my thoughts. Perhaps…he fed them to the sharks?"

The duke shook his head, and walked on.

I returned to work, but the woman would not release her hold upon me. Staring blankly at a blowpipe, I recorded its details without enthusiasm. Standing now, I stretched, and ordered myself to force her from my mind. *You have important work to do*, I reminded myself.

Seated again, I noticed another plait had undone. It was with considerable relief that a knock on the door presaged the arrival of Tommy, with my luncheon. He appeared as agitated as ever, but the threepence he seized with his nail-bitten fingers encouraged him to loiter.

"Tommy, I am in great need of your assistance. Firstly, who is that young woman I've seen about the estate?"

"Tall 'n thin, Suh? Face loik a goddiss? Curly copper head a hair, freckles? Oyes loik shiny emrilds? Smoil loik—"

"That's her!"

"That'll be Farma Cooper's dorta, Ruthy. Plenty a lads uv fought ova 'er. Roit little 'art breaker, she iz."

"*Ruth*, you say? Farmer's daughter? I see. Now, getting back to business, last night a monstrous bird, much resembling that stuffed specimen, alighted outside my room. It then made its way to His Grace's apartment…"

"We've, we've all seen it, we 'av, Suh."

"Is it some sort of extraordinary…pet?"

"And we've all seen 'em dead sheep. Ripped ipart, they is."

"You must tell me what the devil's going on!"

"Oi cun tell ya this: regla's clockwuk, 'is Grace opens win-dah beoind stuffed boyd when 'e locks up a' noight.

Closes it foist thing in mornin'." He was hurrying for the door. "Of all t'win-dahs in this wing 'e could open, it's always that-un—boi that blasted boyd, Suh."

Being unconcluded with my enquiries, I grasped his arm with considerable firmness.

"I need more. *Anything* that springs to mind, Tommy." Recognising his reluctance, I added, "There's a shiny new sixpence in it for you—I'd offer you a shilling if I could, but I'm not being paid to solve this mystery."

"Well…oi can tell ya oi 'erd 'em arguwin' a coupla days afore 'oneymoon…"

"Go on."

"T'dook and 'is bootiful new woyfe—she wuz an angel. Always foun' toyme t'say g'mornin' t'staff, she did. She 'ad a smoyle for us all. She even—"

"Tommy—stick to the point!"

"Sorry, Suh. It wuz day before they caught steamship. Arguwin' proppa loud, they wuz. Oi was-n eavesdroppin', you believe me, don't ya?"

"Of course. Continue, Tommy."

"She wuz croyin', repeatin' ova 'n ova that she wan-ned 'er money spendin' on upkeep o' 'ouse, 'n grounds. She loved 'em plants…wan-ned ta build a 'ooj glass'owse for 'em 'n fill it wi' pri-ee roses. 'E wuz shoutin' 'bout buildin' a blasted mooze-ee-um. Then they wuz foitin' 'bout slav'ry."

"What's there to fight about?"

"T'dook wuz collectin' slav'ry tings. She wuz sobbin', she wuz. She said slav'ry wuz work o' t'devil. She begged 'im ta see it 'er way. In t'end, she said it wuz oither 'er or t'blasted slav'ry stuff. Oive neva seen 'im so angry. 'E wuz shakin' 'n shoutin', 'n then this 'uge purple vein come up…oy thor 'e wuz abouta burst 'is bleedin' brain-box!"

"A big vein, you say?"

"Loik a bulgin' worm it wuz, royt down middla 'is fore'ed. 'E ordad me 'n Jackson t'row t'deepest par o' lake, where we dropped whole bloody lota slav'ry stuff in."

"Thank you Tommy, that's most helpful. You are indeed

a shining star. I will be certain to get that sixpence to you before I depart. On that you have my word."

"Thank-oo, thank-oo, Suh—oil give it ta me mama—she'll be sa 'appy she'll croi 'er oyes out! But please Suh, don't neva tell no one nuthin' 'bout nuthin' we spoke 'bout."[63]

True to habit, he legged it.

Neither the matters with which I wrestled, nor my location, altered over the next hours.

The connection had of course occurred to me, but only a man of unsound mind would have failed to dismiss them, without hesitation, as being utterly implausible. A stuffed bird coming to life when summoned by drums, killing, then returning to the status of an inanimate museum exhibit, at its master's bidding?

How had Professor Reynolds described the duke's thesis? *As bordering on the delusional.* Was it evenly remotely possible that the late professor—a man widely admired for his level-headed and continuous pursuit of fact—was referring to the sequence of events referenced at the end of the previous paragraph?

What precisely *had* the duke learned during his numerous and lengthy sojourns in Amazonia? What dark secrets had the natives of that continent been persuaded to part with for his benefit?

---

[63] Sixty-three footnotes previously, I referenced the potential impoverishment of the language of Shelley, Keates, Tennyson and Shakespeare. With these thirteen words, Tommy threatened our beloved language's very survival.

Another consideration took hold moments after the last: would the sorcery of that unchristian environment remain efficacious six thousand miles away…in *England*?

It seemed most unlikely that the duke would share this information with *me*, a humble cataloguer and aspiring postgraduate. If only I could get my hands on his thesis. Perhaps it lay forgotten in some dark corner of the university's Bodelian Library, deprived of the illumination afforded those works that had satisfied the examiners. Then it occurred to me that rejected theses were most likely discarded—for what academic purpose could they possibly serve? This meant I would never cast an eye over its pages to confirm the delusional nature of its contents.

What was evident was that humour could open no more doors here—what was required was action. I placed two squares of J. Whatman's finest cotton rag paper in my mouth, and chewed them slowly, noting the changing texture. I crossed the room, arrived at my destination, and went about my work. Mercifully, I was uninterrupted.

Returning to my desk, I was certain that the success of my plan required much good fortune...

"My dear Robert—it's as if your mind has been occupied by other matters. Hardly an error all week—and now the album's full of them!"

"I apologise, Your Grace. I confess that my attention has been diverted by a most singular matter."

"Enlighten me."

"If you'd be so good as to observe—you'll notice the plaits of your otter fetish are undoing, yet it remains locked in that glass container. The seal remains intact. There are only…three plaits remaining."

"It's of no consequence. By tomorrow…as I said, it is of no consequence."

I drew a deep breath. "As a student seeking a thesis topic, I am enormously interested in both your collection and your valuable research…it occurs to me that you may have uncovered native practices of which others working in the field are entirely ignorant. Indeed you mentioned the effects of ingesting *Tabernanthe iboga*…"

"You committed that plant's name to memory, yet I mentioned it but once?" The duke studied me carefully. I smiled as best I was able. It was not returned.

"It would be imprudent of me, when I am searching for a thesis topic, not to take heed of whatever snippets of wisdom you are prepared to share. It is apparent to me that you are vastly experienced and knowledgeable, Your Grace."[64]

The duke's eyes narrowed, and his voice deepened. "Continue."

"You described this fetish as of Aguaruna origin…but…and I sincerely hope you can forgive my impudence…"

"Will you kindly get to the point?"

"Well, Your Grace…I'm wondering if there's anything else I can do for you. Any additional work, cataloguing your fine art collection—identifying Stubbs' works, perhaps? In return, perhaps you would consider…"

"You wish me to share my secrets—gathered over decades—in return for your inferior cataloguing? Are you, Sir, *insane*?"

"Forgive me—I had no intention to offend."

The duke's visage darkened. "I should've followed my blasted instincts—yet to meet a man I trusted who didn't drink whisky! Knew you were a wrong'un the moment I laid

---

[64] Edmund Burke opined that flattery corrupts both the giver and the receiver. On this occasion I welcomed my corruption.

eyes on you!"

"I'll try and develop a taste for it—"

"And you dare arrive here with the worst haircut I've ever seen!"

"As an impoverished student, one must save money where one can."

"It looks like you cut it yourself! Ill-fitting jacket. That odd tie's been askew all week!"

I ran my fingers through my hair and straightened the tie.

"Now you dare doubt my description of that fetish?" He was shouting. "Have *you* devoted thirty years of your life to *real* scholarship…waded through leach-infested swamps, dined on thumb-sized pupae? Or swiped your hand across your face to remove a carpet of blood-sucking mosquitos, then collapsed from breakbone fever? Have you had your throat opened by a Nsapo axe, and spent the rest of your life hiding the scar behind an absurd beard?"

"Your slavery collection—at the bottom of the lake—I could hire a diving suit and retrieve it for you."

"To whom have you been talking?"

"It was a rumour…I overheard…back in Oxford."

"It's six fathoms deep, you dolt. I've already lost one man who drowned trying to recover it. Caused no end of problems for me with the constabulary." After pausing, he added, "I suppose it might have helped had he known how to swim."

"But I'm a strong swimmer and—"

"Have you been struck with darts dipped in curare, and barely survived the muscle spasms as you half-suffocated to death? Or eaten plants that make you vomit so violently, that your ribs cracked—in your quest to journey deep inside your internal universe?"

"No, I have not."

The bulge of his eyes, the ejection of spittle suggested that his fury was approaching its apotheosis.

"Have you felt the fangs of the Gaboon Viper pierce your flesh, thrust a knife into its brain, only to watch its lifeless jaws chew its venom deeper? Then experienced an agony greater even than the two dozen lashes across your bare behind your father administered for a single mis-spelling…when you were a trusting, wide-eyed child, in search of nothing more than affection?"

The duke's chest heaved from his oratorical exertions.

"Or sucked pus from your own body, then lain delirious as your blackened foot swelled larger than a ham…as you drifted in and out of consciousness? And in the few lucid moments, watched maggots feast inside the open wound?"

Perhaps now was not the time to describe the acute discomfort I once experienced from a bee sting.

"I should leave," I said, moving towards the door. He growled behind me.

"I will inform Parsons of your impudence! And also the university! I may lodge a formal complaint!"

He pushed me out, slamming the door with such force that the adjacent portraits trembled.

"I do apologise, Your Grace."

"After risking my health, my *life* in pursuit of superior scholarship—they dared reject *my* thesis? Fools, imbeciles, ignorami!"

I resisted the temptation to enquire whether his scholastic contribution advanced our understanding of the human condition.

He pulled the key from his pocket.

"You will leave first thing in the morning."

His face had adopted a deep crimson as he slid the key in the lock.

How had Dr Parsons described his scholarship? As containing *insufficient verisimilitude* and *excessive imaginings*. Though this elegant description explained why it was rejected, something warned me it was better not to reacquaint the duke with this inconvenient detail.

He glared at me, his face smeared with contempt. A great purple vein wormed down his forehead and his eyes bulged so, that I pondered whether, as Tommy had so eloquently contributed, he was *abouta burst 'is bleedin' brain-box.*"[65]

I held my breath as he turned the key. Prayed.

He spun around to confront me. "Now get out of my sight! I will give instructions that you shall not be fed tonight, or in the morning. You will be packed and gone before breakfast. Now go!"

I hurried away, praying the execution of my plan had been faultless—however, I would not know for some time. What I did not anticipate was the duke's last words that travelled down the corridor with such force that it was as if I'd been struck in the back: "You mark my words, young man, and you can pass this on to Parsons and the other charlatans that infest that inferior university. You can tell them that—much sooner than any of you could possibly imagine—I will enjoy the last laugh!"

Battered by maniacal laughter, I bounded up the stairs and crossed the hallway. The sanctuary of my room, evidenced as soon as my door had slammed closed behind me, was as nought, for the cacophony continued to pierce the timber, the wall, and my brain.

The duke was true to his word. Neither Tommy nor a tray of food arrived. It mattered little as the extreme excitement and appalling menu had taken the edge off my appetite. I waited until the sun had set, lit a candle, and grasping the Bible, made my way downstairs.

The broad corridors and portraits made me most uneasy,

---

[65] Revisiting this phrase, I wondered if I had been prematurely dismissive of Tommy's grammatical constructs. Clearly, we all possess some Milton within us.

a state that was magnified by the dancing shadows cast by the flickering light. I passed a suit of armour that appeared to sway, a marble bust that seemed to turn to face me. With relief, I reached the door to the collection.

My fingers closed on the handle, and I turned it. Nothing happened! I pulled but the door held fast.

"Dammit!" I whispered, dropping to me knees to inspect the lock. "It didn't work."

How could I have possibly imagined a sodden wedge of paper would impede the action of a new Chubb lock? My mission lay in ruins. I had failed.

Head in hands, I began to imagine the outcomes—each more serious than the last—that awaited me upon my return to Oxford.

So completely did my misery engulf me that I was not immediately aware of the changing texture of the air. It felt charged with electricity, as it does before a violent thunderstorm. With hindsight, I associated the subtle alteration I experienced in clarity and depth perception with that same elevated pressure.

I heard a click. The door opened. And there she stood.

With the hat discarded, I immediately knew her name was not Ruth. Nor was she a farmer's daughter. In place of copper curls, I marvelled at the waves of gold. The soft blue of her eyes matched the cyan of the artist's palette. Her face was sculpted in a perfect symmetry, and though she smiled, she radiated unfathomable sadness. Instead of freckles, I beheld translucency about her pale complexion; the attendant scent was of damp paperboard. Time slowed as we stared at each other and I would swear on the Bible, that minutes, hours, lifetimes passed. Finally, she walked— perhaps *drifted* better describes her motion—past me and into the hallway. Besieged by emotion, unable to find my voice that I might speak—though I had a million things, and nothing, to say—she faded into the gloom.

Leaning upon the doorframe hoping the dizziness might pass, I bit down on my lip, in order that the sting might return me to the present, and remind me of the urgency of my mission. Finally, I collected myself sufficiently to stagger into the room, where I spied the skull fetish. A single plait remained!

I hurried to the stuffed condor. I read aloud passages I had selected from the Bible that addressed the battle of good against evil—Revelation 12:9, 2 Corinthians 4:4, Romans 12:21.

With trembling fingers, I unwound the linen that bound the bird's head, gasping when the extent of the mutilation was revealed. Of the eyeballs, there was no sign—the apertures had been crudely stitched closed.

Experiencing a need for physical connection with the miserable creature, I rested one hand upon it.

I lifted the Bible and spoke. "Dear Lord, I pray you will release the hold—the control—that the duke maintains over this stuffed bird. I do not understand how he makes it do his bidding, but I know that it must be abhorrent to all Jesus taught and be the work of Satan himself. Please break the bond between the duke and the bird immediately. Amen."

I opened the Bible at Ephesians 4:32. I had planned that Matthew 6:15 and Luke 6:37 would follow. But before I could speak, the drumming commenced.

"Why has it started so early?" I asked the bird. Was that a *tremble* that passed through it, rippling the feathers?

A chill passed through *me* when its head turned towards the open window. "Bird, I have done all I can!"

I fled the room and ran back to mine. When I reached it, I slumped upon my bed.

With the duke commencing the ritual earlier tonight, I had not had time to recite the final Bible passages—the ones that addressed forgiveness. Indeed, I did not know what, if anything, my efforts had achieved.

The tempo of the drumming was building. Standing beside the window, I saw the dark shape flap past.

It hovered outside the duke's apartment. The drumming ceased, the window opened, and the creature entered.

However events would unfold, I knew I had no means of escape from Montagu Hall. If I attempted to make my way down the drive at night, would I meet the same fate as the stag?

Terrible screams shattered the stillness of the night and I rushed back to my vantage point. Lights flashed from the duke's apartment and a shower of sparks sprayed from the open window. Whatever the constituents of the affray within, it contained elements unknown to this world. Shouting followed, but the words were so distorted by terror that I was unable to recognise them. Perhaps they were not English?

Two booms signalled the discharge of a shotgun, but immediately thereafter an appalling cry sent shivers coursing through me. Piteous pleadings followed, and on this occasion I did recognise the words: "Forgive me!"

A crash of furniture followed; it was joined by a lingering wail. That wail transformed into a howl and that howl was followed by a single word that hung in the air until it had tapered away to nothing: "NOOOOOOOOOOOOOOOOooo!"

An explosion of glass.

A sickening thump.

Moaning.

Silence.

SATURDAY – *note to self: at least certain aspects of the matter are resolved, though most untidily. No further concerns, surprises, or horrors could possibly lie ahead…could they?*

At some point I must have slept because I was awoken by a violent knocking upon my door.

"Suh—it's Tommy. There's bin some sorta acciden' but we can't get 'is door open."

"Give me a moment to dress, Tommy." Then I realised that I had not changed into my pyjamas the previous night.

"You alright, Suh?" He asked when he saw me.

"No."

We hurried towards the central block and mounted the grand staircase three steps at a time.

Fitz stood outside the duke's apartment. "Mornin' Suh," he said. "Gard'ner's gone ta get 'is tools. No 'mount o' shoutin' 'n bangin's gettin' a reply from dook's rooms."

As if to prove it, he hammered on the door. "Ya Grace— iz ya in there? Iz ya oright?"

The gardener arrived with a sledgehammer. He set to work with determination. Wiping his brow, he passed the hammer to Fitz. "You 'av a go—God knows what that door's made o'."

Finally, the lock splintered and the door succumbed to our pushes. We entered a chamber that had been much disturbed, with tables and books thrown about. A crushed globe lay on the floor; papers were scattered hither and thither.

Stepping over a broken chair, I arrived at the shattered window. The others joined me there, and we peered down. The duke's body lay on its back, within the confines of the walled garden, spread-eagled upon the plants it had crushed.

We stared at each other.

"So, so much blood…" I said.

"Look a' this!" Tommy picked up a lengthy black feather while the gardener inspected two blast holes in the wall.

"The 'appy couple," Tommy said.

"What?" I asked.

The boy was picking broken glass from a framed wedding photograph. My eyes immediately found the bride. Her gown spilled across the floor; enchanting bridesmaids, bright flowers and broad smiles were scattered about. Beside her stood the duke, who stared fixedly into the camera. Did the upturned corner of his mouth betray a smirk? It took all my strength to hold back a sob. And there, at her feet, sat the dog.

"That's *Barker*, Suh. Runt o' t'li-er—no one wann-ed 'im so she took 'im in. 'E still 'angs aroun' hopin' one day she'll come 'ome."

Emotions welled up inside me. I had been through this before—at my parent's funeral. I had handled it then and I would handle it now. How would my companions respond if I broke down? What would Garnet Wolseley think? I busied myself inspecting objects as if deep in thought, but it was a ruse as I fought to regain control. Just when I feared the battle was lost, an item on the writing desk drew my gaze.

"Weez betta moike sure the body ain't messed with 'n get p'lice over," the gardener said as they departed, the sledgehammer resting across his shoulders.

"I will join you presently," I said.

I walked over to what had caught my eye. A sheet of paper lay beside it on which the following was written: *For the attention of Dr Riley-Roper.* The item beside the note was no slave manifest or pair of manacles; nor was it a whip. Like the catalogue album I had worked on all week, it was bound in black leather and was substantial.

I opened it with care. The pages were filled with writing, artistic depictions and photographs of natives, their villages, and artefacts. Fine illustrations of animals and plants—some lifted with a wash of vibrant watercolour—broke the monotony of the text. The duke's labour was also evident in the liberal use of footnotes that rendered my employment of this referencing convention, by comparison, conservative. The gold wording on the cover read:

A Treatise on the Phenomenon of the South American
"Nagual"
or
By what means a Man may Shape-shift to Assume the Form of a Wild Animal

Re-submitted, *in absentia*, to the Department of Anthropology

of the University of Oxford, in Satisfaction of his Delayed
Doctorate Originally Submitted in 1866
by
Bartholomew Osborne Randolph Ingram-Saville
The Ninth Duke of Dingley
21st June, 1899

I must confess that instead of joining the others with the
haste I had promised, I began turning pages. I had no idea of
the passage of time as my wonderment grew. A shout from
outside interrupted me.

"Everythin' or-roit up there, Suh?"

"On my way," I replied.

Some time later I joined them in person but not in mind,
as I attempted to comprehend the extraordinary subject
matter of the deceased's thesis. I also considered the
significance of the embossed text upon the cover. The first
point was the phrase *in absentia*, which was Latin for *while
absent*; the second, was the reference to tomorrow's date. As
intimated, the recently departed had indeed intended to travel
somewhere tomorrow.[66] But why would he wish to resubmit
his thesis on his late wife's birthday…on the same day that
his collection and walled garden were to be enjoyed by
prestigious academics and their families…and to where had
he intended travelling? And what journey could have possibly
been more important than finally enjoying the satisfaction of
a number of Oxford University academics acknowledging the
quality of his scholarship—a satisfaction no doubt multiplied

---

[66] Though I suspect his travel arrangements had not anticipated a
thirty foot plunge into a walled garden.

when they were compelled to concede that their predecessors had been so misguided in their conclusions?

Tommy's sobbing returned me to the assembled company. He said, "Them oyes—they've only bin gouged out, they 'av. It's too 'orrible t'look."

The gardener shook his head. "'E landed in joy-int 'ogweed. Its sap's loik acid when sun 'its it. Tamorrah 'is skin'll melt off."

"Oh, dear Lord—look!" I said, pointing at the painted eggs secreted about the plant's stems.

The gardener kicked a plant of dissimilar design. "That'uns monks'ood. Deadly pois'nous ta touch. T'fiend plarn-ned 'iz damned eggs there too. And 'ere's poisn oivy 'e grew in green'ouse. This un looks loik that damnable Ozstralian gympie-gympie. Watched 'im grow it—'orrible, 'orrible rainforest plant that makes a 'ogweed burn look loik a moild sunburn."

"Scientific name *Dendrocnide moroides*? The duke described it as *simply marvellous*..." I added, shaking my head.

"If oi spoke Lat'n, Suh, oid tell ya what oi think o' the dook in *that* language, so as ta not affend." He kicked another plant. "The maniac—that un's pokeweed. Dunno what that shrub next it is...but he's bin growin' 'em all in green'ouse and plantin' 'em 'ere these past cupla woiks. And there's eggs 'idden in all 'o 'em."

"That explains the canvas gloves I saw in the wheelbarrow," I said.

"More joy-int 'ogweed over 'ere," Tommy, who'd wandered off, shouted.

"And that one with the pretty berries? Are they...grapes...olives, perhaps?" I asked.

"No, Suh. Deadly noightshade, 'n them red 'n green berries is lords 'n ladies—all 'em pois'nous berries ut looks sa tasty ta t'young uns. There's pois'n 'emlock by t'wall—people think its cow parsley 'n eat it—'e musta wan-ned some o' the ladies ta toik it 'ome for cookin'. Oi don't rec'nise some of 'em damned plants but oi knew 'e was uppa summit. No wunda 'e neva allowed me in 'ere."

I collected my thoughts. "So…the walled garden and painted egg party were a cunning ruse to…"

"There's na need ta say it, Suh…"

"Of course! The Fijian chief and his punishment that impressed the duke. Finally I understand—what could cause a family more pain than harming, killing…the children?

The gardener bound the wrought iron gate with rope. Tommy was dispatched to the main gatehouse with instructions that anyone arriving for the grand opening and painted egg hunt be turned away.

One matter remained unresolved. I grasped the cord attached to the curtain that shrouded the sign above the entrance. A pull and the fabric slid away, confirming the terrible truth.

Seldom have five words affected me so. They read: *The Garden of Deadly Delights.*

Members of Her Majesty's constabulary arrived soon enough and, given the elevated status of the deceased, began interviewing and recording answers in those little notebooks they carry, with great solemnity. At all times they displayed courtesy and professionalism, though it was apparent that much of what they heard shocked them. Even when the feather found by Tommy was demonstrated to fit an interstice in the stuffed bird's wing, the police remained unflinching in their commitment to the use of adjectives including *unbelievable, impossible, Satanic.*

At noon, Dr Parsons and Reverend Carter joined us. After absorbing the content of my briefing—a process made vastly lengthier by their detailed questioning—the pair asked for an inspection of the collection.

It may come as little surprise that the final plait had now unravelled and the hood lay upon the cabinet base. As soon as we had steadied ourselves following the observation of what had been revealed, a constable was summoned.

I take no pleasure in reporting that the item proved the duke's motivations to have been more degenerate that could possibly have been imagined. The object now on display bore no relation to the cranium of a giant otter, for it was covered in deeply wrinkled skin. It was evident that the skull had been removed, and the eyes and mouth had been crudely stitched closed.

It was immediately apparent that what had been advertised as woven sloth hair, were in fact human locks. The long blonde locks of a woman…and where the light played upon them, they radiated a golden lustre. As one we recognised the appalling truth: we were staring at the shrunken head of the late duchess.

"My God," I whispered. "The final item in his blasted collection."

Nor did it end there…

For some time I preferred to explain what we next observed, with reference to the differing atmospherics within and without the glass container. Perhaps the moisture that had condensed inside the head, had finally found a means of escape. Because tears trickled down her cheeks.

The following week, The Oxford Times reported that a specially-convened court permitted the duchess's to coffin be exhumed. When the ill-fated lady's remains were inspected by a doctor, in the presence of the coroner, they were found to lack the previously described wounds initially credited to a jaguar, and then to an anaconda. The head however, was absent.

The coroner recorded the probable cause of death as a powerful blow of a bladed instrument that separated the head from the neck, between the third and fourth cervical vertebrae. A note was added that the state of decomposition prevented identification of a foreign substance found in the liver that may have been a poison or sleeping draft.

At a ceremony conducted by the bishop, the head was positioned in its appropriate location with reference to the body. The coffin containing the remains of the late duchess was then placed in a glossy black hearse. The horses, together with the feathered plumes they sported, were also black, as was the attire of the funeral director and bearers. But there was colour too: it radiated through the carriage's glass windows from the scores of golden-yellow roses that had been scattered about the coffin.

The convoy—that included automobiles and carriages filled with family and friends—left early to reach the church in the small village outside Birmingham, late that evening. There, at a simple candle-lit service accompanied by prayers, hymns, and tears, Golden Rose was laid to rest alongside her forebears.

EPILOGUE

London, 1914

Life could be substantially less agreeable: the leather of this wingchair is as aromatic as it is soft, my palate is waltzing to the flavours of a Glenmorangie whisky. However, I do not assume that the reader will be as grateful for an epilogue as I am for the company of the old friend at my shoulder. With that in mind, I have endeavoured to keep this section brief (though the number of outstanding matters requiring clarification, renders this challenging).

As with the prologue, I offer an inducement to encourage the reader to continue reading, by again offering an unexpected reward at the conclusion.

For several weeks following the events described herein, a number of individuals—namely your author, Dr Parsons, the Reverend Carter, and Mr Simpson of the Pitt Rivers Museum—worked tirelessly in order that illumination might be shone upon aspects of this adventure that would otherwise have remained opaque.

I will commence by immediately addressing perhaps the most critical aspect of the narrative: financial compensation. Fortunately, Dr Parsons met his obligations; regrettably, he proved reluctant to inflate my payment to fifteen shillings— despite my pleadings. In any event, my rent was settled on time. However, such was the pandemonium surrounding the duke's death, I am afraid that the sixpence I had promised Tommy, entirely slipped my mind.

I will go on record to state that for some time, Dr Parsons' underpayment absorbed my thoughts. Nevertheless, I was indebted to him for arranging a meeting with the Reverend Carter, at which the good vicar described the benefits of a life devoted to serving The Almighty. While much of this conversation was familiar to me, it provided the vicar with an opportunity to justify God's reluctance to respond to my prayer for greater financial compensation. The reverend did so sincerely, stating (with reference to Psalm 4:3), that the Lord hears our prayers, but knows better than we ever can, what is best for us (Hebrews 13.5).

When I mentioned that *God moves in a mysterious way*, the vicar smiled knowingly, before saying, "When you are able to accept that truth, Robert, your most important journey can begin."

The next matter involved the condor. It was unanimously agreed that the animals that met their demise about the estate were slaughtered by that bird. The duke had control of the creature's body, while the man's intellect—and blood lust—motivated, even controlled it. Mr Simpson was of the opinion that the duke resided *within* the bird during those flights, and by a powerful sorcery, his and the bird's strength were combined, allowing it to subdue animals which might otherwise have proved too strong.

As a committed *animist*, Dr Parsons believed that all God's creatures possessed a soul. He held that by removing the bindings from the unfortunate bird's eyes, and by choosing a selection of pertinent Bible passages, I had succeeded in freeing its soul from the duke's entrapment. I must admit to blushing when Dr Parsons told me that I had done a wonderful thing. As a wild animal, it was unsurprising that it sought revenge in a cruel but fitting manner.

I recall asking Dr Parsons how long it would take before the bird's soul travelled to its appointed place, to which he volunteered that the Mayan believed the spirit spent several weeks *in limbo*, before making that final pilgrimage. He supposed that during that hiatus the animal remained vulnerable to being possessed once again; of the methodology required to do so, he had no knowledge, compelling me to seek answers elsewhere.

During the night following the duke's demise, Morpheus finally demonstrated a sense of responsibility: I dreamed about the bird. Let it suffice to share that the manacles burst open and the ball and chain fell from its wounded leg. It then soared in the heavens, to join others of its kind. Immediately prior to the termination of that dream, it swooped low and tilting its head toward me, grunting softly. I was able to glean meaning in that avian communication. It said *thank you.*

The third matter, if you will forgive a pun, required some unravelling. It concerned how the plaits could undo in the absence of an external agency. I visited, accompanied by Dr Parsons, the Pitt Rivers. While inspecting the museum's shrunken head collection, Mr Simpson explained that the victim's skin is darkened with charcoal ash. This practice is unrelated to the aesthetic sensibilities of the Amazonian. What the native believes is that the ash locks the victim's spirit, or *muisak*, inside the head, preventing it escaping and seeking revenge. It was suggested by Mr Simpson that such was the duchess's sense of outrage—or perhaps motivated by her great love of life—that her muisak had forced its way through the ash barrier to unravel the plaits, in order to reveal the true nature of what lay within the cabinet. In this way, the duke might eventually have faced justice.

Mr Simpson also proposed that the mechanism by which tears flowed from the shrunken head's eyes might be explained in terms of the same esoteric causality.

Finding it too painful, I chose not to share details of my several ghostly encounters with Golden Rose. I prefer to believe that by opening the door to the collection, the tragic lady aided me in my endeavours to expose the truth. I know not whether the plaits were undone by her muisak, or by her spectral hand.

Oftentimes I have accepted that I will never find a wife. In lonelier moments, I indulge myself that Golden Rose felt what I felt…knew what I knew. All these years later, no other woman has stirred such feelings in me. When encouraged to take a wife, I recall telling Dr Parsons that my perfect woman existed only in my dreams. Whether you choose to describe that remark as *tempting fate* or *foreshadowing*, those words still haunt me.

It was but a small step to conclude that the villain of this adventure, in the form of the duke, had murdered his antecedent. Dr Parsons suggested that Professor Sir Rufus Reynolds' unexplained death was likely the work of the same actor. The archived crime report that I reviewed in Bow Street Police Station omitted any reference to the sighting of a gigantic bird in Bloomsbury that day. My conclusion to *this* day remains that a well-timed push ended one man's life, and set in motion a series of events culminating in another man eventually assuming a dukedom.

The curator proposed that the process of shape-shifting by the Nagual goes through several stages. With each, the individual retains for longer periods of time, the appearance of the beast. Over a number of years—between ten and twenty—it seemed that the duke had reached the final stage: he was ready to *become* the condor. At this point he would have abandoned all earthly things, and spent eternity in the spirit world familiar to the shaman. Dr Parsons suggested that this unearthly location may have been analogous to the realm inhabited by ghosts, or the astral plane described by the Theosophists, (a concept that has also found purchase in the manifesto of the Neo-Rosicrucians). Existing in the spirit world, the duke would have been free of humanity—a state he must have considered preferable to his status, wealth, and marriage to a beautiful young woman.

I believe the late duke had refined his plan over many years. He sought revenge upon the faculty, and wished to house his collection in a museum but lacked both an impressive edifice, and the financial resources required to do so. After he had murdered his cousin, his superficial charm and social standing lured Golden Rose, who was disposed of at the earliest opportunity. The mansion and title were a means to an end, not an end in themselves.

With no heir, the dukedom experienced an ignominious termination. D. Westerly & Co. Ltd. was appointed auctioneers. I attended the last day of the sale, and can confirm that while there was a substantial number of lots, no reserves were set, nothing fetched an impressive price, and many items remained unsold. I recognised Double-Fault who bagged a brace of bargains; indeed the modest prices permitted even *me* to depart the auction with a few mementos that I possess to this day.

Montagu Hall was abandoned and fell into even greater disrepair. The land was parcelled off and sold to whomsoever required it. The mansion was run as a lunatic asylum for a period, but the locals joked that the staff soon went as insane as the patients. The last news that reached me was that one of England's finest houses was to be demolished, with rows of modern dwellings planned for its replacement.

As I approach the conclusion of this narrative, I am afforded the opportunity to reflect upon the impact of these events upon myself, seventeen years after their commencement.

Experiences such as these leave few men unaffected and in that regard, I found myself affiliated with the majority. When invited to explain other-worldly happenings, I have witnessed academics retreat behind such erudite words as *positivism, nihilism, epistemology, ontology, phenomenology,* and other *isms* and *ologies* too numerous to mention. Some wisely abjugate the need for intellectual enquiry by relying upon the teachings of The Good Book.

I experienced my awakening some days after the duke's death. Handicapped as I am in my talents as a scribner, it is to the Bard, and indeed his creation, Hamlet, to whom I turn for an elegant representation of my position: *there are more things in heaven and earth, Horatio, than are dreamt of in your philosophy.*

I came to accept that much had been denied me during my formative years, and henceforth, I was determined to observe the world through a different lens. It was Reverend

Carter's determination that that lens share the same optics as his. I evaluated every argument he presented in my search not only for answers, but indeed for a direction in which to point myself for the remainder of my earthly years.

If you will excuse me, I have quite lost my thread on account of a commotion in the street below. A vendor of *The Evening News* is ringing a bell loudly, and shouting with determination, employing alarming words such as *danger, murder,* and *lunatic.* No doubt he is referring to the assassination of Archduke Franz Ferdinand, the heir to the Austro-Hungarian throne.

In fact this ominous news reached me yesterday—who dares predict the enormity of the forthcoming conflict that has been triggered by a Serbian bullet?

May I further indulge your patience? Barely an hour has passed and I have again been interrupted—this time by a knocking on my door.

I called out *do enter,* and Mrs Crawford, my landlady, obliged.

"Good evening, Dr Walters. I wonder if I might trouble you for a moment."

"My dear Mrs Crawford, how may I be of service?"

"Forgive me for bringing it up again, but your room and board are outstanding."

"Indeed they are—I am comfortable and well fed."

Her tone softened. "I mean—you promised to pay me on Monday."

"How remiss of me—please accept my sincere apologies." I extracted a five pound note from my wallet.

"I shall have to return with your change."

"Don't trouble yourself—put the balance towards my account. Just be so good as to bring me another of your excellent teacakes."

"Some extra homemade strawberry jam too? I'm pleased you enjoy my cooking, Dr Walters."

"It will join the others to plug the hole caused by the missing fireplace brick."

She laughed. "Oh, you're a one, aren't you? Gin and jokes—the two things that always gets me in trouble."

"I can vouch for the accuracy of that statement."

"Hush now, Robert. We promised never to mention our little…"

"Carnal solecism?"

"You and your clever words. If anyone ever found out, it would be the end of me and the shock would probably kill Joseph too, what with his weak heart, so I beg you—"

"Which is why, Margaret Crawford, of 24 Sussex Gardens, Bayswater, London, my lips are forever sealed on the matter. On that you have my word."

"Thank you. Anyways, I was wondering if you planned visiting the Toad and Turnip public house tonight."

"You wish to provide me with a key for my return?"

"I hoped to persuade you to stay in. I've just finished reading the evening paper—it's full of news of another gruesome murder. A well-to-do gentleman again, but they haven't identified him on account of his terrible wounds, and because his personal possessions were stolen. His body was found early this morning by the driver of the milk pram, face-down in a pool of blood. And I thought London was a safe place to live! Until they catch the madman, please don't step foot—"

"My dear Margaret, you will notice that my window is open. I have a fine supply of evening air."

I faced the window now. A pigeon alighted on the roof opposite.

"Do you sometimes wish you could simply fly away, and leave your troubles behind, with the ease with which that bird just left its troubles in that poor fellow's hair, Margaret?"

She smiled. "I prefer to keep both feet firmly on the ground. And talking of flying, we need to discuss the matter of that *thing* behind you…with its eyes bound like that. Makes me ever so uncomfortable, it does. I could have Joseph store it in the attic, at no extra charge."

"Pablo is not a *thing*, dear lady. He is a stuffed Andean

condor. Over the years, he's become a friend. Now if you'll excuse me…"

"I was going to mention the drumming. Other guests have complained. You should have seen the state of Mrs Parker's children at breakfast."

"I will try to moderate the noise…you have my permission to punish me however you see fit…"

Her cheeks flushed, and she laughed. "Oh, Robert, you're a one, aren't you?"

I smiled at her, and she giggled like an adolescent.

"*Humor plus aperit quam veritas.*"

"Dr Ever-so-clever, aren't you, with your ancient Greek? My mother warned me about gentlemen like you."

I smiled and she laughed again.

"I best be going before I get myself in trouble," she said, holding my eyes with hers, as she closed the door.

Following her departure, I locked it.

Finally, if I may be permitted to conclude without further interruption: it had long been my goal to complete a doctorate and secure a lectureship at the university. I am proud to report (and my more observant readers will have inferred), that I achieved the former.

Regarding Dr Parsons' three objectives, the examiners concurred that the Alpha—the presentation of an original work—was satisfied.

Following my choice of thesis topic, it soon became apparent that the satisfaction of Dr Parsons' remaining objectives (the delivery of a societal contribution that would have relevance in one hundred years), proved problematic within those pages. However, a solution had already presented itself that Wednesday at Montagu Hall: I would address the societal contribution in an alternative document. That document is the one you now hold in your hands…

Fortunately, Dr Parsons' warning involving the substantial academic commitment required to satisfy the examiners proved inflated. Production of the first draft was tedious—I have never been an enthusiastic copier—but the subsequent re-write involved little more than deleting some fantastical claims and toning down others.

Finally, there was the small matter of adjusting the title. The wording on the cover of the volume that rests upon my knees reads:

A Treatise Examining the Apparent Phenomenon of the
South American "Nagual"
or
*By what means the Natives Claim a Man may Shape-shift to Assume
the Form of a Wild Animal*

Submitted to the Department of Anthropology of the
University of Oxford
by
Robert John Walters, Esquire
14th March, 1902

The modest income of the lecturer and uncertainty involved in the securing of a professorial chair undermined my commitment to pursuing the academic path, obliging me to explore other means of supporting myself. Furthermore, my enquiring mind had been satisfied with both *a priori* knowledge and *a posteriori* evidence concerning that which I previously had rejected or failed to consider.[67] The career I eventually chose guaranteed a ready supply of fine Scotch,

---

[67] Lest this narrative adopt an excessively sombre tone, let me offer the following: *why did the brontosaurus have one brain in its head and a second in its tail? In order that it might think* a priori *and* a posteriori *simultaneously!*

while the work itself afforded me the honour of changing fundamentally the lives of others.

My final words on the subject are these: having survived this adventure, I experienced a profound reversal in my world view, whereby the mysterious became the obvious, and *vice versa*.[68] Having devoted countless hours struggling to understand the death of my parents, I decided that my future would be better served worshipping a deity, aligning with a religion, following a path—call it what you will—that moved in a less mysterious way. Permit me to add that this decision was in no small way influenced by a matter of the heart, to which I have previously alluded.

I am standing at the window observing the throng of bustling humanity in the street below, as ordinary people go about their ordinary lives. Confirming the time on my recently acquired Asprey pocket watch—gold, of course—I see that ninety minutes still separate me from the witching hour. I have just this moment noticed that the delicate filigree engraving upon its back contains dried blood—nothing a little soap, water and scrubbing won't remove.

I recall Margaret Crawford's descriptively fallacious ejaculation, and, without facing the bird, address it thus: "Can you believe, Pablo, that that woman—who remains sublimely unaware that her intellect rivals that of a shoelace—cannot distinguish Latin from Greek? It would have made no difference had I shared that pearl in a more familiar

---

[68] I am surprised that Conan Doyle's jolly escapade *The Hound of the Baskervilles* has enjoyed an extended shelf-life. This may be explained, in part, by a thought-provoking line within it: *the world is full of obvious things which nobody by any chance ever observes.*

vernacular: *humour opens more doors than truth.* Its pertinence would still have escaped her...as it does so many.

"For the past seventeen years it has been child's play for me to demonstrate that if you make them laugh, they will like you. When they like you, they cease to think—so seize every opportunity to amuse, I say! Soon your quarry becomes as malleable as that curiously popular import, Wrigley's Spearmint Chewing Gum. This analogy extends further: like gum, they must be spat out when no flavour remains."

After a brief gestation period, I added, "Did John Lyly not propose the sentiment that *all's fair in love and war*?[69] Well, only a fool would propose that life is not war."

A tremble of feathers indicated that the bird had awoken.

"Do the giggling Margaret Crawfords ever realise when they have been—I believe the popular word is—*played*? Will it ever dawn upon the trusting reader who else has been included in my (I predict) enduringly relevant experiment?"

Which brings me to the fate of this manuscript. Should it find its way into the hands of a publishing house that deems it worthy of a modest print run, I would be obliged if a copy be delivered to my *alma mater*, Balliol College.

No doubt it will collect dust on a remote shelf of that great institution's fine library; perhaps spiders will spin webs about its cover.

Were I to indulge myself, I might imagine that one day, before its pages are blackened by mould, or it is discarded to make space for a worthier tome...a student may alight upon it.

Perchance he might interrupt his studies long enough to browse its contents. Whether that student becomes a soldier, sailor, tinker, tailor or even Prime Minister, I would

---

[69] Indeed he did—in *Euphues, the Anatomy of Wyt,* published in 1578. You will be relieved to learn that this is the final footnote—on that you have my word.

encourage him to employ the wisdom proffered herein, in order that it might serve his ends, as it has served mine…

Furthermore—

Confound it! I find myself interrupted by additional knocking—and it sounds most urgent! The accompanying shouting is in a decidedly vexed baritone.

"Dr Walters—are you all right in there? I've never heard such a commotion! I demand immediate entry!"

"All's well, Mr Crawford. Why do you ask?"

"I have to say, Sir, you were making the very devil of a noise. You've woken Mrs Parker's children again and they are howling. I very much doubt they will sleep now."

After pondering this unjust accusation, I said, "Noise, Sir? I am engaged in writing."

"Writing, Sir? You were engaged in *laughing,* the likes of which threatened to cause my heart to seize. For the first time in years, Mrs Crawford has been forced to open the gin bottle to calm her nerves."

"My dear Mr Crawford, there must be some other explanation."

"I demand you open the door without delay, Dr Walters."

"That won't be necessary, and in any event, I am already in bed."

"You leave me no choice, Sir: we shall discuss this further in the morning."

When the footsteps had receded, I faced the condor.

"My dear Pablo, I trust you are in the mood for a crepuscular homonym: my wallet has lost five pounds. Consequently, I am wondering if you would care to join me at midnight for another night on the town. I can promise that as always, it will be the most entertaining portion of the day."

The bird wheezed.

"What's that you ask? Ah, *crepuscular.* It means twilight. By now you will have learned that a man of my elevated acuity would never limit himself to the vocabulary of the commoner. What? Oh, the homonym. You see five *pounds* could refer to a sum of money, or to a weight. Clever, don't you think?"

The gentle snorts that followed were laden with despair.[70]

"Indulge me, Pablo! And as before, we will comb the ether tirelessly for *her*. Unfortunately, it has proved to be rather crowded there; fortunately, neither of us is limited by time..."

I paused to accurately articulate a thought that had recently matured into a conviction, "...though a nagging concern invades my mind in unguarded moments: I fear that we may be searching for my beloved in entirely the wrong location. Sadly, we are both aware that the Pearly Gates would never open for *our* kind."

I responded to Pablo's nodding with a deep sigh.

"So be it, my friend. And you know what else occurs to me? Were the valiant Major Dalton present, he'd state—his back ramrod straight, his glass eye watering—that I have greatly disappointed him, by failing to develop into the shining star he'd expected of me. He would—"

The bird bucked its head and grunted.

"I do wish you wouldn't interrupt so! Though I feel compelled to add that I never cease to marvel at your intelligence. Not for the first time I find myself in complete agreement with you, Pablo. As you so eloquently put it...not all stars shine."

---

[70] Another footnote, you ask? Could anything matters less than an untruth—large or small—if it performs a usefulness?

ATTRIBUTION

The use of footnotes throughout Golden Rose prevented me attributing material in the conventional manner.

Information regarding Scottish tweed (footnote 20) was sourced from the website of that marvellous shop, Campbell's of Beauly: https://www.campbellsofbeauly.com.

www.wikipedia.org (as published on 31/03/2022) was my research resource for material involving the ethnology, anthropology and etymology of shamanism, and the effects of envenomation.

You Only Die Twice

The Dead Man pressed his back against the brickwork, blending into the shadows of the doorway. His eyes slid left and right. And back again. *Good—they don't know I'm here.*

Emerging, he slipped into the crowd that had gathered on the street corner. Hunched and drab, he knew he wouldn't be noticed by the young, the busy, the colourful. But it wasn't them he feared.

He studied the crumpled body across the road as a cop waved cars by, one by one. They slowed, their occupants craning their necks for a better look. A kneeling paramedic shook his head and a woman sobbed into her hands. It started to rain.

Faces pressed against the steamed-up windows of the pub behind the ambulance. The sign identified it as *The Black Adder*. The Dead Man shivered so he pulled the frayed collar of his coat up to his ears. *Is it still known as "The Bladder"? Whatever it's called now, it's where I met her, sipping a ginger ale—five cubes of ice—studying her sketch book, as she sheltered from the rain. Swirling showers had swept up from the meadow behind the pub that day...just like they're doing now.*

They heaved the stretcher into the ambulance; a blanket covered the corpse. The Dead Man couldn't tell if it was a man or woman but he wondered about the victim anyway: *did that poor soul ever find lasting love? The kind that means that despite the disappointments, the pain, the fear, their life was worth living? How had she put it? Something about days that filled themselves, rather than days needing to be filled. But her words had been more elegant.*

The clouds grumbled closer. The Dead Man stood lost in the Long Ago, until a gust of rain spattered him awake. *An angry sky plus a tragic death? Hardly the right moment for my annual pilgrimage. Best I come back later when things have settled down...*he glanced about, exhaled, and shrunk back into the shadows…*if* they *don't catch me and…drag me back.* The Dead Man walked as smoothly as he could, pacing himself to blend with the others. He used the overhangs, the lampposts, anything, for cover. Every minute he checked he wasn't being followed. *At least they're easy to spot because they always—*

"…kay?"

…

"Are you okay?"

…

A man's voice? Was I struck from behind? Injected again?

"What the hell happened?" he asked.

"You tripped on a loose paving stone. Can you stand?"

"Should we get help?" *A woman this time.*

A couple stood over him. *I don't like how close they are, and what's wrong with my eyes? Why are they all blurry?*

The man offered his hand. "Let me help you up."

Instead of taking it, The Dead Man thrust his hand into his pocket. He found what he was looking for. *Good—it's still there.* The couple came into focus and he forced a smile. *Thank God they aren't White Coats!*

"Don't worry. I'll be fine."

"No broken bones? You've got a nasty swelling on your cheek," the woman said.

The Dead Man touched it. Flinched. "It's nothing."

"You look so cold," she added.

"He'll be fine. And we'll be late," the man said, taking her by the arm and dragging her away.

It was a while before his spinning head cleared and he stood. Dared walk. He touched his cheek again. *At least the blood has scabbed. I've got time to kill—so I might as well see the town. But I must be careful. If I'm lucky, I'll get to come back later to do what I must do.*

The Dead Man passed a couple laughing under a shared umbrella, the rain winking in her soaked hair. He stared at a woman giggling into her phone...her cheeks flushed, her eyes shining. He knew it was rude but she didn't notice him. Few did these days.

A burst of rain forced him into a bus shelter. He rubbed his eyes. Once it helped him see better, but these days it helped him focus his mind. Too stubborn to wear glasses, he struggled to read newspaper headlines, or the time. He checked his wrist but there was no watch there. *I suppose time doesn't matter too much now.*

When he saw lovers, he'd think of *her*. He'd relive the poppy field picnics, the matching shells they found at low tide, the tangled limbs in the summer heat. Exclamation Mark, so spontaneous with his advice, had promised time would heal. *Mark, perhaps you should have stuck to renaming pubs.*

He exhaled until he felt pain, as if emptying his lungs would refill his heart.

After all these years, why can't I let go?

He thought of the meadow; her running barefoot through the tall grass; the pastel of wild flowers, the dancing butterflies...he dabbed at his eyes. *You're only making it worse. As The Brigadier used to say: "Get a grip, man—you're letting the side down."*

"Why's my foot freezing?"

He looked down. *Fool—last week you lost your watch. Now your shoe. Must have been when I fell. Why didn't I replace that lace? I can afford a damn shoelace, can't I? Of course...if I hadn't wasted money on that newspaper.*

The remaining shoe was a black Derby. The uppers were holed and cracked, the sole worn away. Creases on its uppers were as deep as the lines on his face—though they told fewer stories. Over the years, wardrobes had come and gone. But the shoes had never let him down. Like him though, they got few outings these days. But he had to find its twin.

The Dead Man walked back the way he'd come, stooping under the weight of the moth-eaten overcoat that over time seemed to grow heavier, even as it became more threadbare.

Do I turn left, or go straight on?

Would I would have noticed that hardware store if I'd passed it earlier?

I'm going round in circles.

He stopped, his head dropped.

Shoe, when I get back to The Ritz, I'll stuff that newspaper down you. I'll dry you on a hot radiator and polish you until you shine again. But he knew he needed to cover the old blanket with the newspaper, because he couldn't afford to run the heating.

Maybe there's another shoe hiding somewhere in my suite. I mean, it's difficult to keep track of things in fifteen rooms. Didn't I see a brown one under the chaise longue? Or did I give it to that pretty charity collector? Can't remember. But what I can remember is that she was number 731. Or 732.

My foot's not cold now. It's numb. Numb is good.

The Dead Man slipped his hand in his pocket again and checked the small box was still there. *Box—we know all about numb, don't we?*

A dirty toe protruded through a hole in his sock. He flexed his foot and water dripped off. But he knew the remaining Derby wouldn't let him down. "It's just the two of us now, shoe. We'll have to look after each other," he said.

Now you're talking to a damn shoe?

The Dead Man wondered about the traffic victim's funeral. *How many mourners will attend? The only people who'll come to mine will be the priest and the hole digger.* Allowing himself a thin smile, he whispered, "A priest? Who do you think you're kidding?"

"I married a dead man," his ex-wife used to shout. "You never laugh. Never smile. Wrapped up in your own misery. Yes, a dead man!"

One evening in the Bladder, he repeated this to Duracell Dave, who said Veronica was spot on. Of course The Brigadier and Exclamation Mark agreed...so he'd been known as The Dead Man ever since.

But they're all dead now. How's that for irony?

"And I might as well be..."

The Dead Man wandered up a side road. He wasn't really looking anymore because he knew the shoe, like him, was lost. He was thinking of the meadow again.

Someone was smiling at him so he smiled back. Paisley Afghans billowed over lilac Crocs. Her tanned face—he corrected himself—more olive-skinned than tanned—poked out from under the collar of a vast sheepskin. *As for that hair colour—I can almost hear The Brigadier: "Ye Gods—the young these days! A five mile run followed by an ice cold shower's how to start the day...instils a sense of social responsibility."*

I wonder if that colour has a name.

"Pinkissimo," she said.

"I didn't mean to stare."

"It was Tangerella last week."

She said something about her flatmate being a hairdresser, but he was looking at her eyes: bottle green, with flecks of light.

Fascinating...she could almost be Rebecca's double. "I'm sorry—what did you say?"

"I asked if you'd like me to get some ice for that bruise."

"It's nothing."

"So, we've made this random movie for our final exam…"

864 thinks I can afford a movie?

"Another time," he said. *Another place.*

She was staring at his feet so he tried to hide his socked foot behind the Derby.

"Admission's whatever you can afford…and I promise it's as warm as hot buttered crumpets in there."

"With melted honey?" he asked.

"With melted honey."

He looked at the frayed building behind her. The architecture was Victorian. Or Gothic. Or both. Or neither.

"What's the movie called?"

"You Only Die Twice."

"And it's about…?" he asked.

"Oh, I can't tell you *that*. It would spoil the fun! But you'll have to hurry. It's about to start."

"Any White Coats in there?"

"Excuse me?"

"Shifty looking guys with fake smiles and soft voices, but they're really serial killers."

"It's full of them," she said, her eyes sparkling. "One last thing…"

She pulled out a clipboard and handed him a pen.

"Name, address, signature—you know the drill—for our records, you understand."

"Do I need to read the small print?" he asked.

"Can if you want. But it's just the usual stuff…"

He scribbled *The Dead Man, Presidential Suite, The Ritz,* and looked up.

"You forgot to date it," she said.

The date's about the only thing I'd never forget. "Twentieth of September," he said, as he added it.

He pulled up his coat sleeve to reveal his forearm. He drew an X through the 863 and wrote 864 beside the other crossed-out numbers.

"Welcome to the club," he said.

"Does it have a concierge service?" she asked.

The Dead Man returned the pen and clipboard. He shuffled through the wrought iron gates and into the foyer. It was good to be out of the rain even if the air inside smelled of dust and headaches. He pushed a coin through the slit under the kiosk window. The glass was so dirty and the light so dim that he couldn't see who slid the ticket back to him, but the hand looked young. *Do they all wear black nail polish here?* The ticket reminded him of the tram tickets his father used to collect, frame, hang and bore on about. *But a nice authentic touch anyway.*

864 appeared at his shoulder. "You're lucky. You got the last seat in the house, but they've dimmed the lights. We gotta hurry." She led him by the elbow. *Even nicer touch.*

She pointed a laser pen into the darkness, the light jiggling on an empty seat, low down, far right.

Row F, by the wall. Enjoy!" she said.

The gloom was broken by a vivid red *Exit* sign that lit the top of a door, bottom left. The screen beside it was veiled in folds of velvet.

864 wasn't lying. They must have the heating on full blast.

The place was packed. He found row F and repeated *excuse me*, as he struggled past the seated shapes, knocking legs as he went. No one moved. No one complained. *Excellent—more bruises—a welcome change from numb.*

He slumped in his seat and glanced at the man beside him. Dark overcoat, like his. *But why is he wearing a bowler hat indoors?* He looked around and saw more coats, turned up collars, bowlers. *I can't see anyone's face...*

He turned to his neighbour. "Excuse me, but is this movie…a porno?"

The man didn't respond.

The curtains parted to a duet of unoiled cogs and whirring chains. The projector rattled to life, spearing a beam of light down the length of the auditorium. Subtitles, corny music. The film was shot in black and white—but that was okay. *Good old-fashioned cellulite. Celluloid.* It opened with a shiny house under a blue sky hissing with arcing swifts. The cars on the drive were shiny too. The V8 that pulled up, burbled. A grand cedar cast its shadow across a tennis court where a couple pranced and laughed.

He sighed. *Our house was like that. Was ours brick? Or stone? Whatever. But it felt like that one.*

Memories came: some happy moments there, to be sure. *Well, there must have been.* But shouting and tight faces too. He wiped his handkerchief on his sweating brow and focused on the onscreen images. He rubbed his eyes. No, the film wasn't out of focus—the place was full of steam that rose off the wet coats. *Warm room plus wet clothes produces moisture equals damp wool smell. But what's that other smell? Sort of…metallic?*

The film's hero was in his family dining room. *Hardly Oscar material.* The boy seemed cautiously happy. It was his parents The Dead Man didn't like. Too strict. Too right all the time.

"Go to your room!" the movie-father shouted at his son. *Sounds familiar.*

But The Dead Man was losing interest. *At least it's warm—maybe too warm. I'm sorry 864—but I'd leave if I wasn't hemmed in.* He closed his eyes and when he dozed, more memories came:

"You've been seeing that Rebecca behind our backs!" His father shouted. "You promised—"

"Yes, you promised us, young man!" his mother added.

"I never promised. I'm twenty-three—stop treating me like a—"

"Don't you dare use that tone of voice in *this* house! Next you'll want to *marry* her! What will the O'Connors think? Sean and Maeve will never invite us over again," his father said.

"And what exactly do you suggest I tell Father Gallaher?" his mother asked, voice ascendant. "You know any children you have can't be baptised?"

His father's ended the argument with: "I'll deal with this. Trust me, you'll thank me one day."

Damp wool flooded his senses again. He thought of Rebecca. Bottle green eyes lit with flecks of light, raven curls so thick, so soft. *How different things would have been if we'd defied them.* Because for as long as he could remember, he'd known he'd have to marry the Right Answer. *Their* choice. Veronica.

The Dead Man studied the steam rising in the theatre auditorium. He checked for the box in his pocket, then opened his coat to release some heat. He unbuttoned the top of the flannel pyjamas he wore under the coat, lay back and fanned his face.

The movie droned on. Our movie-hero slumped against a window as a postman's van departed. He collapsed in a chair, a letter falling from his hand. The Dead Man gulped. *Believe me—I feel your pain.* He looked down, willing the scene to end.

The words *"There will be a five minute intermission while we change reels"* flickered on screen. The lights came on and a young woman in a billowy scarlet dress and white shoes, walked down the aisle. A tray, supported by taut shoulder straps, jutted from her waist. She turned to face the audience. *Very 1960s—or 1950s—or 1970s. A nice touch, whatever the decade. And if her nose was bigger, she could almost be 865.*

Despite the ice creams and soft drinks, and her flashing smile, no one moved. The Dead Man looked around. Just row upon row of black coats, turned up collars, bowler hats; and that coppery smell again. He leaned away from his neighbour. *Have you tried Listerine?*

He was thinking how similar 864 was to Rebecca—but different too. Like in a dream when you *know* it's your mother but the face is too round, or it *feels* like your car but the colour's all wrong.

He'd heard that Rebecca married a man of her faith. They said he was an actuary. *How did Duracell Dave describe actuaries? As accountants who couldn't stand the excitement. And she, of all people, married one!*

Swallowing didn't soothe the lump in his throat.

The lights dimmed and the screen sputtered back to life.

Now our movie-hero was at work, trapped in a job his father had forced him to take, trapped in a room with his shouting boss. *I know "trapped".* Our movie-hero walked out, turning his back on his career and family.

I thought 864 said this would be fun.

He pictured the ring. Way more expensive than he could afford, of course. But he'd watched Rebecca's eyes as they'd hovered outside *Samuelson's? Sanderson's?* Whichever. That's how he knew it had to be a platinum band topped with a solitaire. *What was that slogan? Oh yes, "a diamond is forever"...which means this thing has hardly even started.*

He remembered how he couldn't wait to see Rebecca's face when he slid it on her finger, though the band was slim and the stone small. He'd picked the perfect spot on the perfect day in the perfect meadow. They'd agreed it was safer to arrive separately, so he'd left his shoes against the boundary wall as a sign—*you couldn't do that now—not that anyone would steal this shoe!* They'd walk, picnic, then he'd propose as they lay hidden in the long grass under the fronds of an old willow.

I waited for you until dark, Rebecca. You promised your parents didn't know about us, but someone told them. I never forgot his words. He forced them out, "Trust me, you'll thank me one day."

Seven years later the phone rang—Rebecca said it had taken her weeks to track him down after she ran out on her childless marriage. He told her he'd separated and his parents had disowned him. They arranged to meet the following week. Of course there was only one place they *could* meet. The headline still haunted him: "Police Search Woodland for Abducted Woman." Shoulders shaking, The Dead Man choked back a sob.

When he looked up at the screen, an old tramp wandered wet streets. The Dead Man tensed. *A house like my family home—but at the same time different? 864, who looks like Rebecca but with weird hair? Hot buttered crumpets with melted honey— Rebecca's favourite? The movie-hero and his love forced apart; he walks out of a job and now, as a destitute old man, wanders around—wait a minute—this is* my *story! What the hell's going on?*

He glanced at the rows of stationary coats. "Is this a dream? A nightmare?"

He jumped up.

"Let me out," he muttered again and again, as he struggled to reach the end of his row of seats.

The Black Coats didn't move. He stumbled against legs, caught his balance. Clambered on. The Black Coats stirred as clammy hands reached for him. He felt weight, not grip. He tried to scream as he dragged himself free, but the sound died in his throat. On he lurched, until he reached the aisle. One by one, The Black Coats were standing now, shuffling towards him. He limped towards the closest exit: the one under the red light.

The Dead Man stopped in front of the glass-panelled door. Condensation misted the panes. His fingers closed on the knob. Before he pulled the door open, he hesitated as The Black Coats came closer. He rubbed at the moisture, stared through the glass.

Flames danced on great knobbly spheres of dark energy that rotated like the meshed gears of an abominable crushing machine. A door opened in the distance. Through it, limbs flailing, a man pitched forward, fell. The Dead Man leapt back when he heard the crunching, the stifled scream.

He spun around to face a line of advancing Black Coats.

I'm slow, but I think I'm faster than them!

The Dead Man barged through the group of Black Coats; bowlers fell to the floor. He ducked under groping arms, stomping on a felt hat as he ran up the aisle towards the door he and 864 had used earlier.

Bursting through it, he staggered down the corridor, reached the foyer where the kiosk was shuttered yet the lights still blazed. Clutching at his chest, he spun around. *Thank God they aren't following me—and I thought The* White *Coats were the problem in this damn town!*

The Dead Man checked in his pocket. *It's still there!* He kept moving, buttoning the pyjamas and coat as he brushed past a woman in the theatre entrance. She blew smoke in his face. Choking, he descended the steps. *Same height and build.* Another *lookalike?*

What in God's name's going on? Maybe I'm finally ready for the funny farm.

He slowed.

Wait a minute. It must have been when I fell. He rubbed his cheek. *Bang on head plus super hot room equals hellucinations. Hallucinations? I think I prefer* hell*ucinations.*

He stopped walking.

Wait a minute! Maybe…just maybe…some students wanted to scare me. The movie 864 talked about wasn't the one I was watching. I get it now—it was just coincidence she looked like Rebecca. I mean, I've seen so many women who remind me of her that I keep score and I'm up to 864!

And the plot? Riches to rags, lovers torn apart, lives ruined. Hardly original.

He checked up and down the street.

Were they filming me *reacting to a practical joke,* me *being scared rigid with some clever special effects thrown in? Of course—those bowler-hatted zombies were dressed-up students! No wonder they didn't run, didn't grab me. They* wanted *me to act terrified, get to that "door to hell"! Maybe open it…step through. But what I saw through the window must have been some sort of video playing behind it. That makes sense, doesn't it?*

The Dead Man smiled. That *was their film project! Now they'll show it on that internet thing and the whole world will laugh at me. At least they don't know my name.*

Looks like the sky's finally clearing. He checked around him. *No White Coats in sight. There's still time to complete my pilgrimage.*

The day isn't over yet!

But why did they pick me*? Duh! Because—no one gets sued when a nobody dies of a heart attack! That form 864 made me sign? I bet it said I consented to whatever happened to me.*

He laughed. *I may be old, but you know what?* "I'm still in the game!"

His fingers closed on the box in his pocket. *Maybe it's time to sell it. I could buy some new shoes and blankets. I'd have enough left over to use the heating this winter. Maybe I'll finally move out of The Ritz.*

Now concentrate or you'll get lost again. So…where's The Bladder? The Dead Man crossed the road. His breathing had slowed; his heart had settled. He inhaled deeply, until the taste of the movie theatre was replaced with traffic fumes. *You know what? We all need some stimulation from time to time. Keeps the old grey matter in tip-top shape.*

Turning a corner, he found the pub. The police and ambulance had gone, the rain had stopped. Something lay in the gutter where the body had been. He walked over.

The Dead Man knew what it was before he lifted it. The blood had oozed into the shoe's creased leather. The frayed lace hung broken. His hand came up to his mouth.

What the…?

He stared into the distance as he thought and thought. *However I break it down, there's only one possible explanation. Of course!*

Laughing, he wiped the shoe. *Fake blood!* He put it on, granny-knotting the broken lace.

"Oh, those students are good—but I'm better!" *They must have been following me. They found the Derby and placed it here knowing I'd come back. No wait—it was that man and woman who pretended to help me when I tripped. He coshed me, she stole the shoe when I was out cold.* He looked about him, searching for a hidden camera. *As I suspected, they weren't the Good Samaritans they pretended to be.*

"I know you're filming me!" he shouted. "Forgive me if I ruin your epic movie, but I'll find your hidden camera if it kills me!" He inspected the screws of a road sign, studied the top of a lamppost, the branches of a tree.

His gaze settled on a figure across the street. *There's a Black Coat over there! Look how suspiciously he's behaving.*

"I've spotted you!" The Dead Man shouted, but The Black Coat pulled his bowler down and hurried away.

"Not so fast!" The Dead Man shouted as he rushed into the street. Horns blared, a taxi swerved. A car clipped his hip and he fell. Another crushed him and the shoe spun into the gutter. A woman screamed.

"…kay?"

…

"Are you okay?"

…

A man's voice? Was I struck from behind? Injected again? "What the hell happened?"

"You tripped on a loose paving stone. Can you stand?"

"Should we get help?" *A woman this time.*

The blurred couple stood over him.

The man offered his hand. "Let me help you up."

The Dead Man rubbed his face. *Wait a minute!* They came into focus. "I know who you are—leave me alone!" He staggered to his feet.

"No broken bones? You've got a nasty swelling on—" the woman said.

"Get away from me!"

"He'll be fine. And we'll be late," the man said, taking the woman by the arm and dragging her away.

The Dead Man watched them leave. He looked back to where The Black Coat had been standing. *Where is he? I must find that damn Black C—there he is!*

He limped after the dark figure in the distance.

"I know your game!" he shouted, *but I'm faster than you!* Breathing heavily, he clutched at his heart as The Black Coat disappeared down a side street.

"Damn—of all the places he could choose—he's heading for The Ritz!" *I can't risk it—the White Coats'll see me—drag me back—but I* have *to find out…*

The Dead Man used shop awnings and shadows for cover as he followed The Black Coat down the narrow street. He turned away from a passing ambulance, pretending to check the time on his wrist.

Another few paces!

The Dead Man caught The Black Coat by the sign in front of The Ritz that read *Mental Health Facility – No Unauthorised Visitors.* He grabbed The Black Coat. Forced him to turn. Stared into his face.

The Dead Man caught his breath. "My God—promise me that's m-make-up!"

He kept The Black Coat between him and the grey building with the meshed windows at the end of the street, ensuring he was shielded from the two White Coats standing by the parked ambulance. He glanced over the Black Coat's shoulder. *Are they looking this way?*

Gripping The Black Coat's lapels, he asked, "Where's the camera hidden? Is one of these buttons fake? Tell me!"

Instead of answering, The Black Coat emptied his acrid breath into The Dead Man's face.

Coughing, The Dead Man checked again. The White Coats were staring at him! One was pointing. Now they were hurrying towards him.

Damn—I've been spotted!

He shook The Black Coat. "You know what? I've got more important things to do than waste time on your stupid movie. But you can tell your pals—"

The White Coats were closer now.

"Hey you! Stop right there!" one of them shouted.

"Forget it!" The Dead Man said, releasing The Black Coat before hurrying back the way he'd come.

The Dead Man was smiling as he reached the main road. *Those students think they're so clever, but I had the last laugh!* As he approached the pub, the young, the busy, the colourful smiled back. A couple passed arm in arm. He saw their light.

The Dead Man came to a low wall that separated the pub's car park from a lush meadow beyond it. He stood quite still now.

So…here I am again. Is this my sixtieth, or sixty-first pilgrimage here? Does it matter?

A distant willow jutted through the thinning mist.

Rebecca, I know it wasn't your fault you never came. Sometimes life presents us with battles. And no matter how hard we fight, we just can't win…

…but I've brought it with me again.

His head fell forward and he sniffled into his coat sleeve. He dropped to his knees. *I can't do this anymore. Why do I keep coming back?* Shoulders shaking, he sobbed into his hands. He looked skyward, his cheeks glistening with tears. "You know what you can do with your damn *"get a grip"*, don't you, Brigadier? You can shove it—"

"William?"

He froze because he hadn't heard his name in years.

He turned.

She wore a sheepskin over Paisley Afghans. Tears welled in her eyes as she lifted the Pinkissimo wig and let it fall to the ground. She shook her head and raven curls poured over her shoulders.

His voice was no more than a whisper. "But…?"

She took his hands in hers and he stared into bottle green eyes flecked with light.

"I-I don't understand…I mean—"

"Shhhh."

"I don't know what to believe anymore," he said.

He followed her eyes down to the shoe, which shone in the evening sun.

"But the creases, the holes? It looks brand new," he said. "I'm afraid I lost the other one."

"We don't need shoes where we're going."

She ran her fingertips down his unlined cheek, over where the bruise had been.

"And you look brand new too, William."

"It's been so long," he said, his voice catching. "I nearly gave up a million times. I—"

"I'm here now," Rebecca said.

They left their shoes by the wall and hand in hand, stepped into the meadow.

The ground was wet, but warm. They smiled at the dancing butterflies as the tall grass brushed against them. They approached the willow.

Sparkling raindrops dripped through the tree canopy. He parted the fronds and they entered a shrine of blinking lights.

William pulled the faded blue box embossed with gold from his pocket. He flipped the lid to let the scattered sun warm the platinum band. And as he lifted the ring, the solitaire woke, flashing its brilliance on them.

Old Dan and the Key

The boy on the dock knew there were two kinds of luck: bad and very bad. As he watched the ebbing tide carry the sargassum weed away, he knew it might as well have been carrying away his dreams.

He'd read that the Spanish had a word for the worst kind of unlucky: *salao*. And he knew that The Old Man had gone eighty-four days without a fish. Charlie had gone seven. But if he couldn't catch a big fish here in the Florida Keys, how could he even pretend to be a fisherman?

He threw the unused shrimp, mushy from the heat, at his new friend—a pelican he'd named Mrs Summers—that hung around the fish cleaning station at the end of the dock. All afternoon the bird had nodded its head, wagged its tail feathers and got in the way, until he'd relented.

Charlie smiled at the bird. "Persistent, aren't you?"

The shiny sport-fishing boats, with their fighting chairs and spotting towers had returned an hour ago. Photos were taken of pink tourists grinning beside their catches. The mates had filleted the kingfish, the mahi-mahi, the yellowtail and thrown the carcasses into the water as the captains chatted with their clients, hoping for another booking. Charlie had watched the little fish tear at the remains that jerked back and forth as they sank.

"They biting today?"

Charlie turned to face a man who was fumbling for a ringing phone. The man checked it, frowned, slid it back in his pocket.

"No," Charlie said.

"What you fishing for?"

"D-D-Dinner for three."

The man pointed a bottle of Wild Turkey at Charlie's eye. "That's some shiner, son."

Hilarious! How many times have I heard that line today, this week? With red-blue changing to yellow-black, Charlie knew he had another month of this. He knew, because it wasn't his first black eye. With his *salao*, it wouldn't be his last.

"I w-w-walked into a d-door."

The man swigged from the bottle. "Not from these parts, are you. Vacation?"

"From New York," Charlie said. "We rented a condo for t-t-two w-weeks."

"Anyone warn you about Old Dan? Listen up: Whatever you do—don't fall in," the man said. He peered at the water, stroking the white stubble on his chin. "As God is my witness, I saw that brute cut a gator clean in two with one bite."

The phone rang again and this time the man answered it. "I didn't hear it, dearest." He winked at Charlie before continuing. "Not one drop all day...but yes, I can *hear you* loud and clear, Donna! Okay, okay...on my way. I was just talking to—" He looked at the phone, tutted and slipped it away. To the whole world he asked, "How does she do that? A man goes for a healthy walk...it's like she's standing behind me 24/7."

"Is Old D-D-Dan a shark?" Charlie asked.

"What? Oh yes—Old Dan. A crummy shark? I'll tell you this for free: he makes the sharks here look like cuddle toys. Later, kid, I've been summoned." He was some distance away when he shouted, "And keep back from the edge. Old Dan can jump twenty feet straight up to sink his fangs into you."

A drunk thinks he can scare me, after what I go through?

Charlie's thoughts dragged him back to school, again. *What turns someone into a bully? A year ago we were friends.* His teacher had run up behind him before he could slip through the gates. He'd turned his head, hoping she wouldn't see his eye.

"Oh, Charlie, not again. May I say something?"

What's the point?

"Yes, Mrs Summers?"

"Before you can understand Bogash, you need to understand...*yourself.*"

She'd handed him a small book. The cover was stained and faded. "Charlie, I think you'll enjoy it. Remember that whatever it means to you, is as valid as the interpretation proposed by some brilliant Pulitzer winner."

Like I'm some sort of book critic.

"Will it help me understand myself?"

"You can tell me next time I see you."

The drone of a mosquito brought Charlie back to the Florida dock, to the heat, and to the fact he hadn't caught dinner. Again.

He stared at the lighthouse on the horizon and wondered about the drunk's story. *Who is Old Dan? What is he? You took my mind off things for five minutes, mister—but two weeks from now, I'll have to face Bogash again.*

Charlie's mother met him at the door of the condo with hugs and smiles. "You just made me five dollars, young man. I bet your father you'd be late and...oh, don't worry...looks like pizza again."

"I t-t-t-tried," Charlie said, staring at his feet.

"Tomorrow you'll catch a humungous grouper that your father will throw on the BBQ. We'll invite those nice neighbours with the cute daughter. She looks about fifteen too..."

"And I d-d-dropped my phone in the ocean. Now it d-doesn't even t-turn on."

"Which explains why you didn't answer my calls...I would've been getting worried if I didn't know you so well."

"Hey Charlie, trust me—luck changes," his father called from the living room. He added, "I've got three yellowtail fillets in the freezer if it doesn't."

The pizza was okay. In a got-soggy-in-the-box kinda way.

"Strange thing…" his father said, "…I was in the clubhouse after my not-too-shabby nine-over-par, seeing it was like a blast furnace out there." He bit on a crust. "Apart from a framed Tiger Woods score sheet, the walls were covered nose-to-tail with *fish* trophies. In a *golf* club! There was even one of those fish with a sail on its back…is that the same kind as in your book, Charlie?"

"That's a sailfish. The one in the book's a marlin. A giant marlin, so huge it t-t-t-towed The Old Man's skiff for *three* d-days! It was a hundred t-t-times stronger than him but somehow he managed t-t-to—"

"Strange thing was there was this big gap on the wall—no fish, no golf memorabilia. Just a fancy plaque underneath. It said *Old Dan* on it. My new golf buddy Bill, said—"

"W-wait a minute—Old D-Dan?" Charlie asked.

"Apparently he's a barracuda and they're keeping that space on the wall for when he's finally caught. But he's no ordinary barracuda. No Sir! He's a freakish huge monster that lurks at the edge of your worst nightmares. Lives somewhere near the dock. So clever no one can catch him but one guy came close. He gaffed Old Dan through the eye but the gaff broke. When the committee heard about it, they named a sand trap after him because it gobbles up anything that gets too close. I should know. It cost me the match."

"I heard he bit an alligator in t-t-two," Charlie said.

"Bill said he's got teeth like golf tees. There's no escape for fish, seabirds—apparently he's so spiteful he bites turtles' flippers off for fun.

Charlie imagined a torpedo, motionless on the seabed, teeth glinting. Maybe Old Dan lived in a deep hole, perhaps his lair was hidden by a mass of mangrove roots. He'd wait for hours, days. Watching. Calculating. Still as death. An unwary fish swims by. A flash of silver, billowing sand and…another victim swallowed whole.

"Marlin are noble fish. Strong. Beautiful," Charlie said. "Old D-Dan's a coward. I hate cowards," He picked up the tattered copy of Ernest Hemingway's *The Old Man and the Sea* and headed for his room. "See you t-t-tomorrow."

"Why not stay? There's a movie starting in ten," his mother said.

"*The Strange Case of Dr Jekyll and Mr. Hyde,*" his father added.

"What's it about?"

"It's an oldie about a doctor who creates a potion that transforms him into—you sure you don't want to watch it? I don't want to plot spoil."

Charlie shook his head.

"Well, it transforms him into a wild, uninhibited murderer called Mr Hyde. But he isn't some Frankenstein created by a crazy scientist. It's about what's evil *inside* Dr Jekyll, which is brought to the surface by the potion," she said.

Just her sort of movie.

"I think I'll go read about catching a monster fish."

"Must be the fourth time he's read that book," his father said when Charlie had gone.

"Look me in the eye and convince me you didn't make that barracuda story up. I mean, ripping off turtle flippers! You should be ashamed of—"

"From Key Biscayne to Key West, Old Dan's a Florida legend; up there with key lime pie, margaritas and sunburn. But in front of a grand jury, if I didn't plead the fifth, I might admit to omitting a trivial detail. Bill said the fish probably died years ago."

"So why keep a space on the wall for it? And that stuff

about *noble* and *coward?* Never heard him talk that way." She smiled. "I hope that story fires up his imagination. Maybe it'll stop him worrying so much…"

"…about Bogash," his father added.

She sighed. "If it weren't Bogash, it would be someone else."

"Truth. And believe me—he's not changing school again. You gotta hand it to his new teacher—what's her name?" he asked.

"Tina Summers."

"She chose a great vacation read. Must know he loves fishing—I mean he's been watching every video he can about it here so that—"

"Have you ever watched him fishing?" she asked.

"Why?"

"He just sits there staring at the water. Zones out completely," she said.

"He's trying to work out where the fish are."

"My intuition tells me he's looking for something besides fish."

"Like what?"

"Who knows?"

"What I *do* know is that my intuition tells me never to argue with your intuition," he said.

At the sixth yawn, Charlie placed the book on the bedside table and clicked off the light. He imagined The Old Man fighting the giant fish for three days. *Three days!* He thought of Bogash and tensed. *7.7 billion people in the world and he had to come to my school. Nine hundred kids to choose from but he bullies me.* Then he remembered Mrs Summers' words: *Before you can understand Bogash, you need to understand yourself.* He rolled over and pulled the pillow over his head.

He tried to think about fishing but Bogash returned.

What's to understand? It's simple: He despises anyone different. And having a stammer is very different. *Thanks for the book, Mrs Summers. Yes, The Old Man knew everything about fishing. But did he know anything about Bogash?*

The morning sun warmed Charlie's back as he paced the dock. *It's good to be alone—not listening to them arguing about that old movie over the waffles and Tropicana. Why does Mom always bring up her therapist and bore on about the "unconscious mind"? If we do have some sort of monster in us—for once I'm two-hundred percent with Dad on this one—we should kill it! Stone cold dead, and the sooner the better! But it's like she wants to cradle it in her arms, stroke its head, introduce herself to it, because apparently it's part of us. Blah, blah, blah. What was the fancy word she used—the one that made Dad yell?*

He checked his watch, studied the strength of the current.

"Integration." That was the word. So you integrate with your monster and live happily ever after. Remind me to mention that to Bogash. Should do the trick.

He unfolded tide tables, ran his finger down a column of numbers.

If I could catch Old Dan, maybe the golf club would buy him off me to mount. Would I make the news? He imagined the headline: *Schoolboy Catches Record Barracuda. Maybe it would go viral—what would my classmates think? What would Bogash think of me then?*

He stepped off the dock and walked towards what Hurricane Irma had left of the old stilt house at the end of the channel. He calculated the shadow cast across the water by the mangroves at different times of the day. Though scratched, his Polaroids pierced the glare so he could distinguish deep water from shallow, movement from stillness. A small nurse shark undulated past.

"Hey, shark—I've g-got an idea. You ever see that movie T-T-Trading Places?"

When the shark had gone, Charlie took a few steps, stopped, shook his head. *Not enough cover. Current's all wrong. Dan needs more depth.*

He walked a hundred yards beyond the dock. *Wait a minute. If Dan only has one eye...that means he's lost his binocular vision—judging distances will be difficult. Catching fish—almost impossible. Yet he's survived—he must be smart. Maybe he feeds on the fish heads and carcasses swept down in the current from the cleaning station.*

A cut in the channel caught his attention. It was framed by thick mangroves and veiled by the branches of a gnarled tree. The spiralling eddies stilled in the darker water there. *That must be a deep hole. In fact...it looks very deep. The current will carry things right into it. Then they'll sink to the bottom.*

"Bingo!"

Charlie turned to confirm what he already suspected: With no cover behind him, he stuck out on the skyline. *Old Dan's down there watching me. Even with one eye, he misses nothing. Cunning, aren't you? But you don't know I've found you, do you? When you're mounted on the golf club wall with my name on the plaque...maybe then the salao will finally end.*

An empty soda can circled in a back eddy. As Charlie wondered about the slob who'd throw their diet coke in the ocean, it sank. *I was right. The fish heads will end up on the bottom here too.* Mrs Summers flounced over to say hello but paddled away, her bill tossed high, when he didn't feed her.

Charlie tried to focus. He pulled off the Polaroids, cleaned the lenses, and looked again. *The shadow's a problem—it always is—but...is that a log on the bottom?* He dabbed at a trickle of sweat before it stung his eye. *If that isn't a log, could it be...?*

He gasped. *He can't be that big!*

A cloud took his light.

Can he?

As he sat waiting for the cloud to pass, he thought again of the last day of school. He'd been hurrying between classrooms. Charlie turned a corner and *crash!* He collapsed, groggy in the aftershock of the explosion. Bogash's size 12s straddled his head. Jack said he'd punched Charlie. Scarlett thought he'd used the back of his hand. To Charlie, it felt like he'd been head-butted by a piano.

"Hardy-har! What's teacher's pet gonna do now?" Bogash shouted. Charlie knew what was coming.

"I'll t-tell y-you w-what th-the n-n-nerd's t-too sc-scared t-to d-d-do: t-to g-g-get up a-a-and f-f-f-f-f-f-f-f-f-fight! That's what!" Bogash was still laughing as Charlie wiped Bogash's spit from his face.

Charlie blinked back to the present, to the dock, to the heat. He exhaled through clamped teeth; unlocked his fists. *You're in Florida now. He's...not...here.*

"Lupo! Lupo!"

A woman strutted past. "Have you seen my darling Lupo?" She fanned her face. "Pink poodle, diamond collar."

"There's a huge barracuda out there. I hope he d-d-didn't go for a—"

"Swim?" She paled beneath her Palm Beach suntan. "He knows he's not allowed to swim on his own. Come to Mommy. Lupo, where are you my darling?" She shrilled her way toward the pool area.

Charlie stared at the barracuda's lair. "So, D-Dan...what'll it be today? A kingfish head? Bonito guts? No one tell you all that junk food's bad for you? Maybe I can tempt you with something special for your last meal on Earth."

As Charlie slept, he shared a skiff with The Old Man—a speck on the cobalt blue of the Gulf Stream. The Old Man talked of the lions he dreamed of, about a baseball player called *The Great DiMaggio*, and of epic battles between fish and men.

Then he taught Charlie how to set the baits. "If we catch a fish this far out, it will be huge," The Old Man said. "You will help me kill it, Charlie."

"Do you kill all the fish you catch?" Charlie asked.

"Of course."

"Why?"

"For food. And for pride."

"It's okay to kill them for pride?"

The Old Man was watching the lines that disappeared into the prismed deeps.

"Are the fish we catch our enemies?" Charlie added.

"No. Because they are a part of us, like the ocean is a part of us."

Charlie crawled towards the channel in the dawn gloom.

He unwrapped a parcel of kitchen foil and lifted the fish fillet. He wove the largest hook he had—sharpened last night—through it, and raised the rod to cast.

Wait! This isn't any barracuda. It must have seen a thousand baits. I need to be smart. Didn't The Old Man cover the hook points with sardines so the marlin wouldn't feel the sharp steel?

Charlie shook a bag of shrimp onto the grass and chose the largest. He broke off its head, and slid the body over the hook, so it curled around the bend, covering the point. Then, lying on his back so his silhouette wouldn't alert his quarry, he cast. The bait splashed up-current of Dan's lair. Charlie waited, his finger touching the line so he could feel if anything ate the bait. He pictured it fluttering deeper and deeper as the current carried it towards the hole. Towards the monstrous barracuda.

The Old Man had set his lines between forty and 125 fathoms. *How deep is the hole?* Whatever the depth, he knew he must concentrate to ensure the bait was exactly where it should be.

How am I doing, Old Man?

The line stopped moving. *Good. It's sunk in the right place.*

Charlie waited. *Bogash will ambush me again in front of the class. No one will help because they're scared of him. How can I win? Why am I thinking about him when I should be concentrating on catching the biggest barracuda in Florida, maybe the world?*

He waited. *If I was listening to Mom, she'd be saying how The Old Man fished all alone in the deepest water, and caught a giant—a creature from another world.*

A cormorant landed on a mooring post and spread its wings to let the sun dry its waterlogged feathers. *What if the little fish tear my bait apart before Old Dan finds it? I should have brought a spare.*

He waited. *The Old Man was smarter than the marlin but it was much stronger than him. He managed to fight it to the surface and kill it using all his knowledge. Is that what the story's about? Brains defeat brawn?*

A sport-fishing boat burbled past. The cigar-smoker in the cockpit rubbed sunblock on his giggling girlfriend as Charlie stared at her micro bikini. *If only I could catch a big fish for dad to BBQ. But forget it—the angel next door would never be interested in a misfit like me.*

He waited. *Okay, so I'll stay with how Mom talks a bit longer. What if you do think of the ocean differently? An endless, deep, dark world we know little about. Full of giant fish, giant squid, giant things—many of them dangerous, scary. Like she said—what if you thought of it like the unconscious mind? The Old Man battled and defeated a mysterious giant that lived its life hidden in the depths—you could go through your whole life not knowing a fish like that existed. But The Old Man won because he understood it better than it understood itself. What if—*

The pull on the line was so light it may have been caused by a clump of weed. But Charlie concentrated, just in case. *That's prime yellowtail, Dan. Firm and tasty. When last did you eat anything other so good? Go on. Eat it!*

The line went slack.

He dropped it. Come back, Dan! That's not just any *piece of fish. When my parents find out where it came from…*

Dan returned with a gentle pull. Charlie felt the weight

on the line as the fish moved away; then he felt tapping, as the barracuda turned the bait in its mouth before swallowing it. Charlie counted to ten, braced himself. With a deep breath he swept the rod back to drive the hook home. He struck again. The rod doubled over.

"T-T-Take that, Dan!" he shouted.

What the...? The line held fast to the sea floor. Nothing moved. *That's no barracuda! Has a moray eel dragged the bait under a rock? Is the hook stuck in that log I saw yesterday?*

The log moved.

Then the fish charged down-current, tearing line from the reel. *Only one fish moves that fast.* Charlie sprinted along the skyline as he tried to keep up. The fish stayed deep. It doubled back, sweeping back up the channel.

Yes, you're strong, Bogash. The fish shot past the dock towards the marina, the line hissing through the water. *The Old Man fought the marlin for three days, so fish, don't expect me to give up any time soon.*

The angle of the line told Charlie the fish was near the surface. Would it jump?

Charlie remembered his favourite passage in the book, when The Old Man had gripped the thick fishing cord as he crouched in the skiff; how the ocean had bulged ahead of the marlin before it jumped. Charlie pictured it coming out of the water unendingly, with the sun warming its purple back and lighting the lavender stripes on its flanks.

Jump, so I can see you, you coward. Go on jump! And the fish did, with a clumsy crash.

"Barracuda d-d-don't g-grow *that* big!" he whispered. *But you are no marlin, Bogash.*

The fish turned and raced down-channel again, shooting past Charlie. He ran after it as it made for the open ocean.

He's heading for the stilt house. If he wraps the line around a stilt, the line'll break in seconds. Of course you'd like to hide under there. Stay out in the open, fight like a man!

Charlie knew he couldn't stop the fish reaching the stilt house. Wait—the marlin was much stronger than The Old

Man, but The Old Man had won. What would you do now, Old Man?

Come on Einstein—think!

He wiped his forehead; caught his breath. The fish rolled on the surface with the line only feet from a barnacled stilt. When the fish had recovered some strength, it would swim towards the open ocean. And cut the line.

There's nothing I can do…

With a sliding splash, the pelican landed in front of him; folded her wings, shook her tail. And stared.

"Any suggestions, Mrs Summ—?"

Charlie froze. *What was that? A…voice?* Was it inside his head or had it carried to him on the same breeze that stirred the mangroves? Slowly he nodded. "Thank you, Old Man."

He lay down and let the line run slack. *Now Bogash can't see me and with no pressure on him, he should think it's safe and swim back this way. Out into the open.*

"Your move, Bogash."

The line twitched. Moved. Picked up speed. Swung back towards him. The fish was returning to its lair.

When the barracuda passed in front of Charlie, he jumped up and wound down hard. The fish plunged and rolled. But like all ambush predators—like all cowards—it had little strength left after the first brutal attack. Lying still all day, it never developed the great stamina of a marlin.

"The size of it!" he whispered. The back glistened like wet coal. Angry stripes ribbed its pewter flanks. The gouged eye was veiled by a milky membrane. And yes, the teeth were as long as golf tees. *Oh no! The hook's hanging by a thread. One surge and Bogash will escape.*

The pelican swam closer. "Stay away, Mrs Summers. It's too dangerous!" Charlie shouted, waving at the bird. But the pelican floated there, watching.

The barracuda wallowed on the surface. *The Old Man killed the marlin with a harpoon through its heart and then lashed it to the skiff. But I don't even have a gaff. I'll have to kill it in the water and somehow drag it out.* Charlie looked around him. He saw rocks, fallen coconuts and a stout stick. He calculated where the barracuda's brain was, as his fingers closed around the timber.

The current turned the fish and Charlie faced its good eye. Black, ringed with silver, the eye followed his movements, as if the monster was trying to understand.

Charlie guessed its length. Its weight. *That's impossible!*

"Hardy-har, Bogash! You still w-w-wanna know what t-teacher's pet's g-gonna do now?"

He lifted the stick high above his head.

But the sharks tore the marlin to pieces. Only its skeleton was left when The Old Man finally got home. So what exactly did he achieve?

Charlie addressed the pelican. "So, Mrs Summers...I'm never gonna win that Pulitzer but here goes anyway: I suppose The Old Man was proud he defeated it—he wanted people—especially the young fishermen—to see that despite his old body, he'd won the greatest battle of his life, because he'd outsmarted the huge fish. But he must have known that a bleeding marlin dragged beside a skiff would attract sharks and he'd never get it home to sell at the market. So killing it was pointless..."

The barracuda lay still as if awaiting death but Charlie hesitated. He studied the sweep of the fins, the forked tail; the tapered head and murderous mouth. When he looked into its eye, it was like staring down a dark tunnel. At the end of the tunnel he saw himself reflected in the depths of the pupil.

"And then there's Mom's stuff about the ocean as the unconscious, and the hidden monster we shouldn't kill because it's part of us... Was *that* what Hemingway was writing about?"

He hesitated.

"I was wrong about you, fish. You're no Bogash. But I think I've figured out who you are."

Charlie lowered his arm. With one hand he gripped the fish's tail. *That YouTuber better be right about an exhausted barracuda won't attack you.*

He leaned forward and poked at the hook with the stick. The hook fell out and the fish rolled on its back. It lay there without moving.

I can't leave it like that. As quietly as he could, he climbed into the water, to stand waist-deep beside the fish.

He righted it and minutes passed as he cradled it in his arms, his hands well back from its head. It lay there completely still, in the heat, in the light, in the silence.

He broke the silence. "My name's Charlie," he said softly. Then he reached forward and ran a finger along its bony head. Its eye pivoted towards him.

"It's good to finally meet you."

He watched the gills pump strength back into its body. The great tail began to sweep back and forth and he knew the fish was ready. He held it a while longer because he felt a bond had formed between them; he sensed the fish felt it too. Finally he released it and with a gentle push, watched it glide down into its shadowy world.

When it had gone he said, "And promise you'll leave those poor turtles alone."

"Hey, it's my buddy from The Big Apple. Caught that monster yet?"

Too early for bourbon, Charlie noticed. *And you look way better clean shaven.*

"I guess it's not your lucky day again, son?"

"I wouldn't say that," Charlie said.

"Listen—God knows how she knew—but my wife sent me to apologise. Afraid it was the Wild Turkey talking. The Old Dan thing? Fake news. It was a bedtime story my grandpa told me when I was a kid. Along with the Japanese cruiser he sank single-handed and the time he won the Kentucky Derby with a broken arm. But Old Dan was always our favourite. He loved to tell how he fought the brute for five hours, finally gaffed it through the eye, but the gaff broke. Truth is, when I'm juiced up, I get a kick out of scaring tourists."

Charlie turned to face the barracuda's lair. Maybe he'd lost his bearings because something had changed. *No…there's the cut in the channel…that is the right place.* Had the sun swung around to play tricks with the light?

"You lost something, son?"

"I'm looking for the deep hole."

"No deep holes over there."

Charlie stared again.

"Listen. I've been walking this seafront for sixty years. I think I'd know. If I don't see you again, safe trip home, son."

Charlie stood watching the passing boats, a diving cormorant and nothing at all as the tide turned. The pelican kept him company.

A yapping poodle dropped a pink ball at his feet.

"Good morning, Lupo," he said, throwing the ball towards the dog's owner.

"Bring the ball to Mommy and don't you *dare* go in the water!"

When they'd gone, Charlie sat as the rising tide carried the sargassum weed back up the channel. This time he was smiling.

The sun was high when Charlie rolled his shoulders and stretched like someone who'd slept too long.

He turned to face the open sea. "I should have told that guy there are 7.7 billion monster barracuda out there," he said.

The pelican nodded its head.

"Oh, right—this is for you." Charlie tossed the rest of the shrimp towards the bird and watched her scoop them up. Then she spread her wings. The bird lifted into the sky and flapped away.

"Thank you, Mrs Summers."

Charlie started jogging towards the condo.

He never looked back.

ALSO BY BEN

Something in the Water ~ a full length novel (113,000 words) ~ available from Amazon in paperback and Kindle.
ISBN-10: 0956581226
ISBN-13: 978-0956581228
Read on for two sample chapters.

Something in the Air ~ the short story (12,000 words) that introduces a key character from *Something in the Water* ~ available from Amazon in Kindle.
ASIN: B0167GZ4YCIS

SOMETHING IN THE WATER

One man. One woman. One chance. No turning back.

On the verge of losing her job, side-lined journalist Teal Douglas is forced to travel to the South Pacific to profile a powerful businessman. But with her almost-but-not-quite fiancé Bear discouraging her every step of the way, she may not be able to save her career or her relationship.

When corporate criminals invade paradise, Teal teams up with former boxer turned marine biologist Perry Stanley to investigate. With the help of an old islander and a wise humpback whale, they discover the true intentions behind the new fishing operations. Teal must then either accept the plum promotion that will save her career or—with Perry—defend the island with more than her life.

Something in the Water is a full length eco-adventure in the soul-stirring collection from Ben Starling.

AMAZON REVIEWS FOR SOMETHING IN THE WATER

☆☆☆☆☆ Indefinible
"Something in the water SOARS!"

"A riveting read, driven by engaging characters that inexorably draw you into their world. The intriguing, fast paced complex plot includes romance, mystery, suspense, drama and world travel, but also explores other realms. "Something in the Water" weaves a spellbinding tale yet is also a powerful call to action to preserve and protect our threatened oceans and their inhabitants. Captivated from page one, I read straight through to the end, amidst laughter, tears, palpitations, and heartache."

☆☆☆☆☆ Jennifer L
"A powerful cautionary tale, an intense love story, and an intriguing mystery!"

"Wow, if any book ever needed a trigger warning, this is the book…if this book doesn't make you tear up, you're a monster. Starling has created a gripping story that is full of adventure, mystery, love, and has a spiritual undertone to remind us that all life is interconnected."

☆☆☆☆☆ Sarah
"Beautiful Novel"

"This novel will lure you in, intoxicate you, and then fracture a bit of your heart. It will be worth it. I promise."

☆☆☆☆☆ Laura@BlueEyeBooks
"Striking themes"

"Whew! This was quite a journey! This book really spoke to me. I haven't read many books that have conservation take center stage so it meant a lot to me for this author to pick that as their main theme. I won't spoil anything but let me just say that you will need tissues for this. The ending is so emotional and symbolic."

☆☆☆☆☆ Alicia R. Bernal
"The Quintessential poem in a love story"
"The book is about life and death. An unforgettable love story that makes a difference, so that reading any other, after this book of Ben Starling could never be the same."

☆☆☆☆☆ Avid Traveler
"I loved that the book is a mixture of everything..."
"A journey that starts on page one and keeps you guessing, praying, laughing right until the last page. I found myself getting swept up in the characters, cheering for some and rooting against others. I loved that the book is a mixture of everything – mystery, romance, suspense, and excitement. Is it a sad book? At times very, and yes, it made me cry. But I also cried tears of joy. Five very well-deserved stars."

☆☆☆☆☆ Lilyana P
"Brilliant!"
"Author Ben Starling weaves 3 plots together, all of which drive this incredible story forward at quite a pace. Something in the Water is an incredible experience with an unexpected ending, and powerful message. It's funny, sad, interesting, informative (about our oceans) and very exciting and one to go to the very top of your reading list. Can't recommend higher than that! Well done, Ben! Easily worth 5 stars."

☆☆☆☆☆ Amazon Customer
"A storming five stars all the way!"
"A story that transports you to a tropical paradise - or is it? - and keeps you guessing page after page. Great pace,

characters, writing and it left me thinking about our attitude to the oceans very differently. Whether you read this for fun, for the love story or to learn, you won't be disappointed. A storming five stars all the way!"

⭐⭐⭐⭐⭐ M. L. Downs
"Heart Filled Book"

"I ended up crying for the oceans, the whales, all sea life, for the planet, for the lost ways of the elders and ancestors…for all creatures, including humankind, upon this earth. But there is hope, as you say, that life is death's dreamtime. And the one thing that means much to me is when Fonu says, "Sand is time's way of reminding rock who is boss.""

⭐⭐⭐⭐⭐ Tanya Sousa
"Important Environmental Themes, some Interesting Twists"

"I most enjoyed the environmental and spiritual themes in the story that were gracefully woven through a romantic mystery…it's a book that will make you think about your impact on the environment and/or will leave you feeling understood if you already share the ideals within it. I felt understood and kindred. It's also a tale that might make you ask if you are settling for less in your life than you should."

⭐⭐⭐⭐⭐ soughton
"Brilliantly written story……more please!"

"I found Ben's writing style easy and relaxed - which made for easy enjoyable reading. The characters are totally believable and his indepth description of them and their surroundings made me feel that I too was a character within the story. The story line is well thought out and connected all the way. A thoroughly enjoyable read and I can't wait to read more books from this author."

⭐⭐⭐⭐⭐ OutandBack

"A friend recommended this book as a good holiday read"
"Its title was intriguing and it didn't disappoint. It's an action packed story! There's a good romantic plot which is played out against a backdrop of threats to the marine environment. Many of the characters are highly likeable and upbeat, including some of the sealife too."

⭐⭐⭐⭐⭐ **Amazon Customer**
"A real wake up call"
"This environmental adventure is fast paced and absorbing from the off. Twists, humour, love, excitement, angst...and a great set of characters. A real wake up call about our precious and beautiful oceans. A well deserved 5 stars."

⭐⭐⭐⭐⭐ **J. Clarke**
"Romance with a message to all who love our planet"
"I smiled, laughed and cried. It is a story that continues to remind you of its message even when you have finished reading. There are some wonderful lines that sneak their way into your mind, beautiful descriptions and diverse characters."

⭐⭐⭐⭐⭐ **Kindle Customer**
"Inspiring Read"
"Something in the Water is an amalgam of learning to communicate on many levels, evolving and maturing emotionally, and infinite hope. The setting is sublime. A touch of fey brings thoughtfulness and hope. I cannot recommend this book more strongly."

⭐⭐⭐⭐⭐ **Brittany**
"From the soul changing Teal, to the depth of Solomon and the emotions you will feel, you must read this book!"
I look forward to reading more of his work.

⭐⭐⭐⭐⭐ **Amazon Customer**
"Everyone needs to read this engaging novel."
"…I must share that these characters become real human beings living, loving, crying out for justice and compassion in a beautiful world of the sea and those whom inhabit her depths. This isn't just a novel about a woman, but of a good man, of good people changing a part of their world. Personally I found Teal's journey to self-respect, and becoming a woman of strength is one to be envied. And, Solomon's journey between two worlds was amazing and compelling. Thank you Ben Starling for taking me there."

⭐⭐⭐⭐⭐ **Danielle Tara Evans**
"A Very Powerful and Emotional Book"
"This was a very powerful and emotional book to read. At first, it seemed to be a fairly light story, but then its depth was revealed. And there were some very dark moments later on…the suspense kept me hooked, and then of course, it got me thinking about how humans are destroying the oceans and hurting and killing the animals that live there. Highly recommended."

⭐⭐⭐⭐⭐ **SR362**
"A Romance With A Message"
"Something in the Water is beautifully crafted. Yes, this is a love story. Yes, it is a story of a woman who finds herself and what it means love and to be loved. But, this is no simple romance. Starling clearly has a passion for environmental conservation and as a reader you can feel the urgency of it as his words bleed off the pages, touching the reader. Okay, so what's my bottom line. Just that, I loved this book."

⭐⭐⭐⭐⭐ **Roger Sprong**
"Not Just A Romance For Sure!"
"Something In The Water isn't your average romantic story. The author's passion for environmental conservation

provides a background for suspense, surprise, love and a little bit of magic along the way."

★★★★★ Sandra Jackson
"A Clever and Well Written Story"
"Something in the Water is a clever and well written story full of mystery, romance, and characters you'll love to hate."

★★★★★ C. Craig Coleman
"Delicious ocean romance mystery"
"The characters are clearly developed contrasting the New York culture with the ancient culture of the islands. Environmental issues are woven in this fabric throughout as well. This is a delightful read I highly recommend."

★★★★★ abigail
"Awesome!"
"Omigosh - marine-life, conservation, drama and humour! What an assortment of reasons why Ben's writing is classic. No spoilers in this review, but a great big thumbs-up is necessary. Looking forward to more from Ben."

★★★★★ Christy Bunch
"Love story, suspense, mystery and excitement. A great book to read."
"A love story with suspense, magic, old legends and mystery. Something for everyone. Great descriptions of ocean life makes you feel as if you are there."

★★★★★ Lindi
"This is a wonderful book, brilliantly written and researched"
"I have told a lot of friends about the book, and they all love it! Thanks Ben...please write more of these!"

★★★★★ **A Pattenden**
"Heaven on earth?"
"Prepare yourself for the unexpected. Ben Starling has woven a fast-paced tale that works at several levels: relationships, spirituality, environmental. None dominates and the result is a hugely emotional and powerful read. 5 well deserved stars."

★★★★★ **Miroslava Petkova**
"Highly recommended"
"Ben Starling's Something in the Water is an epic story that made me laugh, cry, rage, smile and importantly, think. I learned a lot about our oceans and can't recommend it highly enough. A fantastic read."

★★★★★ **EJ Scott**
"Enjoyed it and will read it again"
"A compelling romance that's also an eco-thriller. Enjoyed it and will read it again."

★★★★★ **georgi**
"An amazing book"
"Enjoyed this book tremendously - it's way more than a romance. More a mystery/thriller with an important message. Highly recommended."

★★★★★ **Tegan Greenway**
"Made me laugh and cry"
"Very well written, felt the emotions of each character and the descriptions put you right into the setting. Highly recommended."

★★★★★ **Amazon Customer**
"Conservation love story"
"A charming love story with a serious message about conservation."

★★★★★ jaye marie
"Haunting story with a message..."
"Apart from the fact that Something in the Water is a cracking good story, the author manages to get the conservation message across in such an easily understood way."

★★★★★ A Riley
"This is a perfect description in the broadest sense
"Something In The Water is a fast-paced yet thoughtful read. I was particularly impressed with the fact that the author, as a male, wrote the compelling character of Teal in the first person. It requires a remarkable amount of insight into the female perspective to write credibly as a female, and he pulled it off very well. I very much enjoyed this book."

★★★★★ Cortney
"I'm not sure if I loved Lizzie at first"
"This was well done, and I do sincerely recommend this to others! I am actually going into my recommends challenge for one of my groups and sending this to my challenge partner!"

★★★★★ chevin
"A great read!"
"Ben Starling's love of the ocean and the environment come through strongly in this book. He has cleverly woven a romantic theme with a fight against polluters in a story that is difficult to put down."

★★★★★ ESB
"Highly recommend"
"I loved this book from the very beginning, and couldn't put it down. The story is wonderfully engaging, but with a powerful environmental message."

★★★★★ Amazon Customer

"High recommend"
"Very helpful important messages from this book
Great job Ben Starling !!! I am very happy to have your book
!!!"

☆☆☆☆☆ **Margaret F.**
"A grand story with driven, interesting characters"
"There's a strong environmental message mixed with
mysticism in a beautiful blend of spiritual tradition and
scientific knowledge. The description overall was lovingly
drawn and quite evocative, especially in the boat and ocean
metaphors. The many cast members came to life on the
page, both those who cared and those who did not, making
for fascinating, realistic people…"

TWO SAMPLE CHAPTERS FROM:

SOMETHING IN THE WATER

CHAPTER ONE

New York, September, 2013

He didn't look like the hotel guests, the business people, or the tourists. He didn't move like them either.

He brushed past me as I climbed off my Vespa, stilettos in hand, outside the entrance of the Waldorf Astoria. Had he smiled at the radiance of my scarlet ball gown? Or was he amused by my battered Converse sneakers?

As a valet approached to take my scooter and helmet, I spotted my boss, Malcolm, waving hello from the lobby. He was approaching the glass doors that separated us when I noticed a small wooden box on the ground. Two steps later, I had picked it up. Who could have dropped it?

No one was close by, so I turned. The only man who'd passed me was already a half block away, gliding beside the cars that waited for the lights to change at the end of the block. Was it his?

What I knew for sure was that now wasn't the time to be tracking down the little box's owner. I should hand it in to reception and concentrate on the evening ahead. For a few seconds I relaxed as I studied the hotel's confident, soaring opulence—a world unknown to me before my arrival from Nantucket four years ago. The smooth texture of the box, however, drew my thoughts back to it. Was there something valuable inside? What if it *did* belong to that man, and he never returned to collect it? I turned the box over—and caught my breath.

"How on earth…?"

Malcolm emerged in front of me. "Hello, darling, you look absolutely—are you okay?"

I thrust my sparkly evening shoes into his hands and hitched up my shawl. I was about to give chase when a convertible Ferrari lurched to a stop beside me.

"Going my way, babe?" its driver shouted, over the thrum of the engine.

But my dress was redder and I got the better start.

The Ferrari leapt forward and the driver middle-fingered a BMW, triggering a duel of blasting horns that ricocheted around the street. I was sprinting now, with Grandma's trusty evening bag bouncing under my shoulder. I weaved between the oncoming gowns and dark tuxedos that ambled toward the hotel's art deco entrance, a stride…two strides…three strides ahead of the Ferrari, with my scarlet shawl streaming behind. Surprised glances. Someone called, "Teal Douglas?"

"Sorry—can't stop!" I answered, without turning.

The man I was chasing didn't seem to be hurrying; *preoccupied* was the word that sprung to mind. But he certainly covered the ground quickly, without apparent effort.

He slipped around the corner onto East 50th Street. The traffic was building and I could see the evening throng thickening, bolstered by more guests heading my way.

Out of sight now, there was a real danger I'd lose him. Then I realized what a fool I'd look if I caught him and the box wasn't his! So I glanced at it again, at the scratched writing on its underside. Yes. I hadn't imagined it.

Turning the corner, I side-stepped an old lady and without slowing, scanned the street. Ahead, a taxi door slammed. Was that him—in tan chinos, navy dock shoes? Or had he crossed the road and disappeared? Instinct told me he was in the cab, and I went with instinct. But I mistimed a dodge and the shriek of rending fabric brought me to a sudden stop.

A blushing jogger stepped off the hem of my dress.

"Hey, Lady! Where's the fire?"

I didn't dare look—I knew the tear was bad. Then seeing the taxi ahead, I called out, "Wait! You dropped this!" with the box held high.

I looped the torn tails of my gown over my arm and rushed on. For twenty strides, the gap closed. Then a delivery van changed lanes and the cab pulled out.

Another shout and the passenger turned. Yes, it *was* him! Strange...he heard me over the roar of the traffic? Though low in the sky, the sun threw a band of light across a face with an expression that blended surprise with humour. A face I'd rather like opposite me tonight, at the Annual Musculus Media Awards dinner. But now my dress was torn, my hair messed up. I felt hot too. I mouthed *Please stop!* but, as if in slow motion, the taxi and its passenger were swept away.

Catching my breath on the street corner, I ignored the staring passersby and fiddled with the torn ends of my once beautiful dress. A window reflection confirmed the bow I'd tied wasn't bad, in fact it wasn't bad at all. Giovanni's salon masterpiece though—my plaited bun—was a disaster. By jettisoning a few hair pins, I was able to restore some symmetry.

Walking back to collect my heels from a bemused Malcolm (and my thoughts), I noticed the box fitted snugly in my palm. As my finger stroked the well-sanded surface, I ran a nail along its snug join lines. When I shook the box, something rattled; despite pulling and twisting, it refused to open. Obviously made with skill, it offered little compensation for my dishevelled appearance.

Why—tonight of all nights—had I been so impulsive? But deep down I knew the answer: I was a sucker for a mystery, and this strange box with the carved writing was right up there with UFOs, the Loch Ness Monster, and relationships that actually worked.

I stopped under the iconic entrance awning beneath the gleaming sign that announced the hotel's name. I dropped the box in my bag to be inspected later, when I wasn't in such a rush. Maybe then I'd discover a pressure point, and it would spring open. Mystery solved. I'd have time to fiddle with it over dinner or after the result was announced. *The result!* I caught my breath as I wondered what awaited me in the hotel ballroom where my colleagues would be collecting, laughing, drinking and discussing...*me.*

Then I froze as people turned and stared. A Rolls Phantom had sighed up to the curb. I backed against a wall to avoid the surge of the crowd. The praying mantis concierge oozed forward, and the chauffeur skipped around to open the passenger door.

"The media magician's here," a man in a tan raincoat beside me said.

"I heard Ronny's onto the old fox—expect a bloodbath," his friend answered.

They dropped their cigarettes and stepped forward. Two dozen more paparazzi jumped to camera-flashing attention. They focused on the older man in the immaculate white tux who slid from the car. Overhead lighting gleamed on patent leather shoes as he applied a three degree correction to his buttonhole rose.

"Basil, look here!"

"Give us a smile!"

"Yo, over *here*, guy!"

He continued to adjust his cuffs and smile until the camera motor drives fell silent.

He delivered a courteous, "Good evening, gentlemen." Spotting my buddy Natalie with her Nikon, he arched an eyebrow and added, "Excuse me. *Lady* and gentlemen."

A voice carried from the thicket of lenses. "Sir Basil, there's a story on the grapevine that all's not quite as it seems at Musculus. Would you care to comment?"

Sir Basil's eyes levelled on the journalist. "Ronny, isn't it? My dear fellow, my interest in grapes and, for that matter, vines is limited to First Growth Bordeaux recommendations from my wine merchants."

"But—"

"Oh, he's good!" The man beside me said.

Had I detected a quiver in Sir Basil's voice? If I had, it was gone when he added, "I'm here for an important annual event, not to give interviews. Now, if you'll excuse me…." He stepped purposefully towards the hotel's main doors.

Taking a deep breath, I darted past the pressing crowd and headed inside.

Let the fun begin.

CHAPTER TWO

If the rumours could be trusted, I was minutes away from the best moment of my life. Words like redemption, validation and recognition jostled for first place in my mind as they had most days since my story broke. But I wasn't celebrating just yet, because I always remembered what Grandma said about rumours: only believe the ones you start.

I studied my Champagne-fuelled colleagues in the splendor of the hotel's Grand Ballroom. Two tiers of gilded balconies wrapped around the room above a stage big enough to handle a Broadway show. Four storeys above the main floor's circular dinner tables, a massive cut crystal chandelier prismed light across the women's evening gowns that glowed with midnight blues, emeralds and golds. The men's somber dinner jackets countered the glinting eyes and sparkling jewels, as their bald pates shone.

A bow-wave of crisp linen preceded my untouched three chocolate soufflé (with wild strawberry drizzle) as I pushed it across the tablecloth. The chefs' lofty accomplishments were wasted on me tonight, thanks to my knotted stomach. Relax Teal. Our charismatic founder and chairman lives and breathes meritocracy and he holds the deciding vote. Keep the faith. Surely they wouldn't overlook you...

For weeks, colleagues had been congratulating me—as if this year's Musculus Investigative Journalism award had already been announced. But with each hearty compliment, another wave of uncertainty crashed through me.

The past year had been a little crazy since I'd jumped at the chance to join the investigative team, following Greg's sudden departure on compassionate leave. As soon as I heard about the vacancy, I knew I had to apply. Some colleagues laughed, others shook their heads or even offered gloomy predictions, but the way I saw it, at long last I was going to be in a position to make a difference. And making a difference was what I'd always wanted to do.

Up until that point, my work at Musculus Media had involved profiling minor celebrities and socialites—not exactly the reason I had gone into debt to attend journalism school, done extra credit in investigative techniques and spent five years toiling for a small town Massachusetts newspaper. But the lure of The Big Apple's lights and a tip-off from a friend about a job opening had persuaded me to take the plunge for the chance to finally use my skills. A chance that somehow never quite seemed to materialize until Malcolm had volunteered me (insisted actually, to his boss in quite un-Malcolm-like tones) for the post. Malcolm the Marvellous who had always championed me at every turn. And it came just as I was contemplating not only the next steps in my journalism career, but in my personal life as well.

This new rung in my career ladder had not been without setbacks but I'd reappraised, regrouped and replanned, using every resource at my disposal (and a couple which, strictly speaking, weren't), to get the story. But I'd done it. And here I was in a city I'd always dreamed about, in one of the most beautiful hotels on earth, waiting to find out if all that persistence, sweat and lost sleep would be recognized.

I let the air escape gently through clenched teeth as I remembered the investment banker who'd been feeding price sensitive information to a hedge fund boss. Both had presented themselves as pillars of society. I wrote about the charities they supported (hosting fundraising events but never putting their hands in their own pockets) and their generous donations to the same political party. It took me months to identify a link between the men but hard work led me to an interesting discovery: they were both members of the same shady "tax efficient" investment scheme. Worth half a billion between them, how much money did these people need?

I looked around the room. Twelve hundred happy, excited, drunk colleagues, many of whom had flown in from all over the Musculus empire. The ethereal waitresses cleared the gold filigree plates and coffee (with cholesterol powdered truffles) was served. I scribbled an extra joke on the eleventh final draft of my acceptance speech that was balanced on my knees beneath the table.

I wondered if (despite what my colleagues had insisted) my story really was that good. Important enough to unseat last year's winner, the unctuous Simon? Well-crafted enough to prevent Deadline Donald from trumping us both on his way to a promotion and office of his own?

A lavender woman from the ninth floor walked over and dropped her hands on the back of the empty chair beside me.

"Edward's working late," I explained. "Financing deadline, contracts to sign, you know how it is."

"Is he the boyfriend from Boston I met last year?"

I nodded.

"Sorry, dear," she said, before moving on.

"Thanks, Edward," I said under my breath. The most important event of my year, probably of my career and I was rolling out the excuses for my partner. Again.

Next to me, Malcolm tilted the MOËT, his thumb buried in the Champagne bottle's concave base. He refilled my glass with a musical May I, darling? and a flourish. His sommelian efforts may have gone unnoticed but the unravelling of his rebellious bowtie was drawing increasingly amused glances.

"Only one glass, I think Teal, if you're planning to ride that death-trap home."

I sipped from my glass. "You're right. I'd better leave Audrey here overnight."

"How are my protégé's nerves?" he asked.

"Let me," I volunteered, as I manipulated the tie's yellow silk. "Despite having the best boss in the world, I'm not getting my hopes up, so I'm not too—"

"Nonsense, Teal, darling. It's a two horse race this year. The Star-Spangled Banner versus the Dis-united Kingdom. Isn't it, Rob?"

"What?" Rob asked, as the woman beside him shrieked. His hand reappeared above the table, curled around an ice cube. Pink cheeked, her cumulonimbus of curls trembled with her giggles.

"Next year you'll be up for a Pulitzer!" rasped Sammie on my left, her sixty-a-day baritone as unexpected as the first time I heard it. "As for that dress—hoping some flashed leg might swing it this time?"

I explained how I'd torn it chasing a guy in a taxi. I fished in my handbag.

"Well, that's one way to catch a man."

"He dropped this," I said, wooden box in hand.

"Whatever's that, darling?" Malcolm asked.

I passed it over. "There's something in it, but there must be a trick to opening it…"

Malcolm winced. "Damn! Thumb nail," he yelped. "Teal, darling, emery board? What do you make of it, Theo?" he asked.

"Locked shut. As mysterious as the Bermuda Triangle," Theo, who sat next to Sammie, observed. "Wait a minute— there's some writing. Left my glasses behind."

Sammie reached for the box. "Good lord! Why's your name carved on the bottom, Teal?"

"I was trying to find out—that's why I chased the guy."

She tried to twist off the lid.

"Darn thing!" Handing it back, she asked, "What do you think's inside? I say a gold ring."

"More likely a bullet," Theo offered. "The clue to an unsolved murder."

Malcolm was sawing away with the emery board. "That's what I adore about my team. You're all so dramatic! It's something a woodwork student knocked together in evening class. Too much glue. Probably his wisdom tooth."

"Anyway, I approve of showing a bit of thigh, especially at a stuffy event like this," Rob said, pulling his chair tight against his date's.

The box circled the table. Now that it was back with me, I dropped it in my evening bag.

"So, what lucky man had you chasing him?" Sammie asked huskily as her cheeks Champagne-flushed.

"Only saw him for a second. I got the taxi number but that won't help track him down."

"Amaze me," Sammie said.

"5728 T1."

"Notice she didn't write it down. Darling, you're simply wonderful! Notice anything else?" Malcolm asked.

"Only the personalized license plate of a Ferrari. GREED E1."

"Ha! Well if anyone can track him down, you can, Teal. God, I got hammered last year! D'you remember?" Sammie asked me, her voice infused with pride. "Keep an eye on me tonight?"

After last year's event Sammie and I'd shared a cab back to her fluffy apartment. Staggering in, I'd used her momentum to tumble her upstairs and roll her onto her bed, scattering her over-nourished cats. We'd discussed boyfriend problems till the early hours and not for the first time she'd suggested that if things didn't improve, I should give up on men and surround myself with felines. A year later and nothing had changed. Well, I had visited the cat rescue website and found their phone number. But I hadn't dialled it yet.

"I remember losing my raffle ticket last year. Only time I've ever won anything!" I groaned. "It must have fallen out at your place, Sammie. Maybe Simba or Garfield ate it?"

"You never told me you won the company raffle!" Malcolm said.

"I came third."

"What was the prize?" asked Sammie, leaning forward.

"No idea. I guess it wasn't meant to be. But—"

"Ladies and gentleman…silence please."

With a jolt, I returned to the present. My knuckles gripped white on the bag. Breathe, Teal. Breathe! I glanced around at the expectant faces focused on the dais. Quiet rippled across forty tables, as indiscretions and flirtations were extinguished in its advance. I double swigged my Champagne (and as no one saw—I did it again).

Above the raised podium, a vast screen flickered to life. The year's highlights scrolled past in a stream of award-winning photos. A banner proclaimed Musculus Media while pulsing speakers boomed Queen's *We are the Champions*.

Our illuminated founder rose from his chair and negotiated the maze of tables, nodding here, shaking hands there, smiling everywhere. His magnified, digitally softened image followed him on screen, together with the legend's legend: your founder and Chairman, Sir Basil Thane.

The room rose as one, cheering and clapping. Rob hurled his napkin in the air and Sammie whooped. A radiant Sir Basil accepted the applause in his gleaming tux, both his hair and teeth looked two shades whiter than last year. His jacket hugged a physique that had claimed an Olympic rowing medal before cinching effortlessly over a claret cummerbund. I had to admit that the Errol Flynn moustache worked alarmingly well too.

Palms raised, I could see few signs of aging in the taught, tanned face—what was his secret, plastic surgeon, or Faustian pact? This corporate icon, philanthropist and devoted family man was rumoured to number world leaders and Nobel Laureates amongst his closest friends; some even claimed he was godfather to a royal prince. As winner of numerous business awards, he continued to wrong-foot the naysayers, the jealous and the merely average in an increasingly cutthroat industry and a decreasingly certain world.

"Friends..." he began and silence fell. "...This has been—despite the turmoil in our sector—a memorable year for us. To each and every one of you, I humbly say..." He paused to lower his head and pyramid his hands in a silent Namaste, "...thank you. Thank you for increasing turnover eighteen percent and profit seven. Every division's performance has improved over last year's, we now have a presence in twenty-two overseas territories and our digital business has grown fourfold in three years. Your company, my friends, sets a standard the rest of the industry can only dream of. Please, feel free to applaud yourselves. Because you deserve it!"

Sir Basil joined in, eye-balling, pointing and thumbs-upping his section leaders. When his gaze fell upon our table, a chuckling Malcolm waved back.

"Some call me old-fashioned, but as a committed champion of ethics, I am horrified that our competitors' efforts remain mired in controversy and criminality." A sip of water and silk handkerchief dab later, he asked, "What's our motto?"

"Instinct—Intellect—Integrity," came the chant.

"I can't hear you!" he said, cupping his hand to his ear.

Theo sighed. "Citizen Thane can't resist showing off, can he?"

We repeated the battle cry three times, each time louder, before he motioned silence. "And friends, I have exciting news. After nearly four decades as a private company, I have taken the decision to sell some Musculus equity. As seventy percent of profits are now US-generated, this will be via a New York Initial Public Offering. Our IPO is in the hands of bankers, lawyers, accountants, PR experts. What this means is that a year from now we'll be a publicly traded company. If we continue on this path of excellence, investors will be clamouring for our shares. Naturally I will be making a suitable percentage of equity available to you, my friends, in an employee share scheme."

Cheering engulfed the room as Sir Basil solemnly bowed. When he straightened up, he was beaming again.

"It's essential we continue to garner our customers' trust. Without it we are just another also-ran. Remember that image is everything which is why I insist on absolute integrity from every single Musculus employee..."

His speeches were usually short, always rousing. My spy in Corporate Social Responsibility had told me to expect something new in his patter this year, right before he announced the winners.

"Helen from CSR has been brow-beating me about our employee-chosen charity scheme. Last year of course, we supported Action on Addiction whose patron is The Duchess of Cambridge—or Kate Middleton as she is known here. And I must say that when I met her at Ascot last season, she was a perfectly lovely young—"

Lady T glared from the front row by the stage. Sir Basil hurriedly shuffled his papers.

"But as many of you know, Lady T has a thing about wildlife in general and Cetaceans—that's dolphins and whales—in particular. You should have seen how steamed up she was when she read that some Icelandic individual was granted permission to kill a hundred and eighty-four fin whales. And he intends selling them for luxury dog snacks in Japan! Never one so foolish as to thwart the wishes of two formidable ladies, I confirm that in a few weeks you'll all be in-boxed inviting you to choose from a short list of wildlife charities."

Polite clapping.

The award ceremony would be next and I gulped from my wine glass. With trembling fingers I lifted my acceptance speech, catching Sammie's eye. Good luck, she mouthed.

"Which brings me to the most exciting part of the evening—our annual awards and this year we have six categories. We will begin the ceremony with Sports Journalist of the Year."

I watched in silence, feeding off the room's heady electricity. When the winner was announced, cheering erupted from a distant table. But my thoughts unwillingly wandered to my mother—and how often she'd told me my sporting successes had counted for nothing.

Rob drifted a question across the table. "Who do you think will win Foreign Affairs this year?"

I missed my colleagues' answers as I scanned my speech one last time. Now Sir Basil was announcing the New Journalist of the Year award. With a shriek, its leonine winner leapt up. Sammie waved and shouted. "You rock, Kenny!"

"Now we come to my personal favourite as I began my career in this field: the Investigative Journalism award. Remember this carries with it a $10,000 prize, which I will personally match with a donation to our first employee-chosen charity."

When the applause had abated, Devonte, the Will Smith clone from HR, stepped forward and handed Sir Basil a gold envelope. I swallowed my way through a wave of nausea. Everywhere I looked, people caught my eye and whispered, Good luck. Malcolm squeezed my arm. What started as a smile ended in a lip bite. Real recognition for my investigative exposé—without doubt the most difficult and rewarding job of my career—rested on the contents of that envelope.

"And this year's runner up, with a superb report on patent-busting in the pharmaceutical industry is Jason Walters. Jason, where are you?"

A roar of applause as an auburn-headed man with matching vest ricocheted towards the podium.

"It's yours, Teal!" Malcolm said.

"Gottabe!" Sammie slurred.

I wiped my damp hands on my napkin. Sir Basil was speaking again, teasing the audience with each precisely enunciated word.

"Choosing this year's winner was a terribly difficult choice. After much deliberation and a dozen recounts (at which everyone laughed)…ladies and gentlemen, the winner of the Musculus Media Investigative Journalist of the Year Award, for the second year running is…"

The gasp that burst from my table stopped me hearing the winner's name.

"What him?"

"Simon? Again?"

"With that story?"

Malcolm, eyes wide, turned to face me. "Darling. This is appalling. I'm utterly disgusted. I was sure—"

I nodded quickly and forced a smile. The walls were closing in, my vision had become misty. I waited until the music started. "Will you excuse me…some fresh air?"

I stood up in what I hoped was an elegant way, then walked with my head held high, ignoring the stares and comments. What did I expect? A fair shot? Life isn't like that. Not in Massachusetts. Not in New York. Not anywhere. Tears stung my eyes but by concentrating on a fixed point ahead, I made it back to the lobby, past the nine tall foot bronze clock there and finally, outside.

Sipping cool air, my pulse pounded in my ears. Was it time to move on? Perhaps I wasn't cut out for this after all. Maybe my story hadn't been so great. But that's not what the whole office had said over and over, insisted a clear voice inside my head.

Go back in there, Teal. March up to the head table, look Thane in the eye and tell him that his directors are a bunch of yes-men and management nothing but two-faced puff-egos, that the spoon-fed Simon couldn't find a story if he typed 'fiction' into Amazon…

"Teal? Teal Douglas?"

"Yes?" I said, jumping.

"I'm Sigvard. Sir Basil's executive assistant. He'd like you to join him at his table."

I should have told him exactly what I thought of his boss. Walked off into the night. Found a job in which—

"Ms. Douglas? Sir Basil doesn't like to be kept waiting."

A NOTE FROM BEN

I hope you've enjoyed these stories which I certainly enjoyed writing. I'd love to hear your thoughts on any or all of them—do drop me a line at benstarlingauthor@gmail.com.

Reviews are the life-blood of authors. I'd be very grateful if you could find the time to review this collection on Amazon and/or Goodreads.

With my thanks,

BEN'S BIO

Ben is an author, multi award-winning public speaker and performance storyteller. He has featured as an expert commentator on the BBC, ITV, Sky News, Sky Docs, BBC Radio World News Service, and on international broadcast radio networks. In 2019, he was selected as a Gold Ambassador by the world's largest public speaking organisation, and also received their prestigious Triple Crown and Gold Speaker Awards. Prior to his work as an author and professional speaker, Ben worked in finance, and as an entrepreneur. Ben graduated from Oxford University with an MA (Oxon), and an MPhil in Management Studies.

CONNECT WITH BEN

Amazon: amazon.com/Ben-Starling
Goodreads:
https://www.goodreads.com/author/show/14246420.Ben_
Starling
Facebook: facebook.com/benstarlingauthor
Linkedin: https://uk.linkedin.com/in/ben-starling

www.ingramcontent.com/pod-product-compliance
Lightning Source LLC
Chambersburg PA
CBHW032011170626
46807CB00006B/2759